What is Indiana Jones doing in British East Africa in September 1909?

He's on safari with former President Theodore Roosevelt. He's watching big-game hunters haul in specimens for a museum collection. And he's on his own quest—for a rare antelope that Roosevelt can't seem to find.

But one thing has Indy stumped. If the antelope is so rare, why shoot it?

Watch Indy as he tackles hard questions, rubs shoulders with America's greatest living hero . . . and blazes a trail through the African bush!

Catch the whole of Young Indy's travels on the amazing fact-and-fiction television series *The Young Indiana Jones Chronicles!*

THE YOUNG INDIANA JONES CHRONICLES
(novels based on the television series)

TV-1. The Mummy's Curse

TV-2. Field of Death

TV-3. Safari Sleuth

TV-4. The Secret Peace

Forthcoming

TV-5. Trek of Doom

TV-6. Revolution!

YOUNG INDIANA JONES BOOKS
(original novels)

Young Indiana Jones and the . . .

1. Plantation Treasure

2. Tomb of Terror

3. Circle of Death

4. Secret City

5. Princess of Peril

6. Gypsy Revenge

7. Ghostly Riders

8. Curse of the Ruby Cross

THE YOUNG INDIANA JONES CHRONICLES™

Safari Sleuth

Adapted by A. L. Singer

Based on the teleplay
"British East Africa, September 1909"
by Matthew Jacobs

Story by George Lucas

Directed by Carl Schultz

With photographs from the television show

RANDOM HOUSE 🏠 NEW YORK

This is a work of fiction. While Young Indiana Jones is portrayed as taking part in historical events and meeting real figures from history, many of the characters in the story as well as the situations and scenes have been invented. In addition, where real historical figures and events are described, in some cases the chronology and historical facts have been altered for dramatic effect.

Copyright © 1992 by Lucasfilm Ltd. (LFL)
All rights reserved under International and Pan-American Copyright Conventions. Published in the United States by Random House, Inc., New York, and simultaneously in Canada by Random House of Canada Limited, Toronto.

PHOTO CREDITS: Cover photograph and interior photographs by Keith Hamshere, © 1991 by Lucasfilm Ltd. Photo of fringe-eared oryx by Jacana/The Image Bank. Map by Alfred Giuliani.

Library of Congress Cataloging-in-Publication Data
Singer, A. L.
    Safari sleuth / adapted by A. L. Singer ; teleplay by Matthew Jacobs ; story by George Lucas ; directed by Carl Schultz.   p.   cm. — (The Young Indiana Jones chronicles ; TV-3) Includes bibliographical references (p.   ). "Based on the television episode British East Africa, September 1909, with photographs from the show."
    Summary: While visiting President Theodore Roosevelt's safari camp in British East Africa in 1909, Indy helps track down an oryx that has mysteriously disappeared.
    ISBN 0-679-82776-5 [1. Adventure and adventurers— Fiction. 2. Safaris—Fiction. 3. Kenya—Fiction. 4. Roosevelt, Theodore, 1858–1919—Fiction.] I. Jacobs, Matthew. II. Lucas, George. III. Schultz, Carl. IV. Title. V. Series.
PZ7.S6155Saf 1992 [Fic]—dc20 91-53168

Manufactured in the United States of America   10 9 8 7 6 5 4 3 2 1

TM & © 1992 Lucasfilm Ltd. (LFL). All rights reserved.

Safari Sleuth

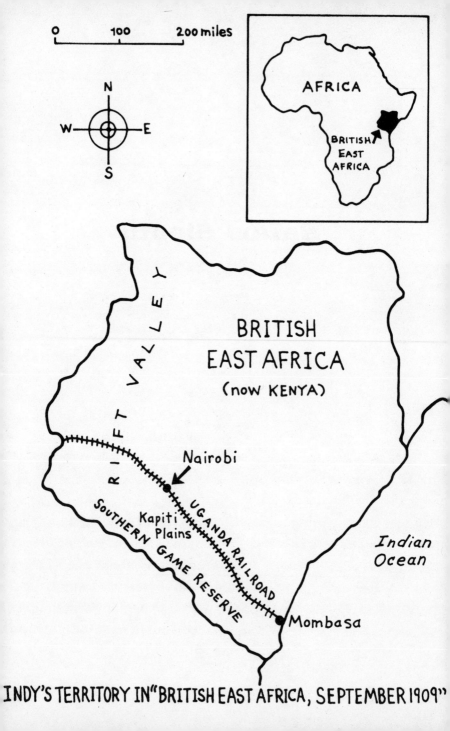

INDY'S TERRITORY IN "BRITISH EAST AFRICA, SEPTEMBER 1909"

Chapter 1

" 'Four lions, two buffalo, ten zebras, five hook-lipped rhinoceros, three warthogs, a saddle-backed lechwe—' "

"A saddle-backed *who*?" Professor Henry Jones asked his ten-year-old son.

"Lechwe," Indiana Jones repeated. "And don't ask me what that is."

A gust of ocean wind almost tore the newspaper out of Indy's hand. He felt his stomach do a flip-flop as the steamship tossed on a swell of water. That was odd. Rough water didn't usually bother him. In fact, he'd been on worse rides during the last fourteen months. Accommodations on his dad's world-wide lecture tour hadn't always been exactly first-class.

It must have been that strange meat he'd had for lunch. "African chipped beef in cream sauce," the menu had said—whatever *that* meant. He'd only been able to stomach two or three bites. He knew he should have had fish, like his mom and dad did.

Well, too late now. Swallowing hard, he folded the paper over tightly. "It says here," Indy continued, "that President Roosevelt has shot all of these animals *himself*, and he's only been in British East Africa since April. That's . . ." Indy counted silently for a moment. It was now September, 1909. "Five months!" he said.

"Impressive," Professor Jones said. "Especially seeing as the old man is blind as a bat and weighs about as much as a hook-lipped rhino himself. He must have emptied seven rounds for each hit—which makes sense, considering what a trigger-happy fellow he is."

Indy was shocked. To him, Theodore Roosevelt was one of the greatest Americans who ever lived. He had done everything—overcome childhood illness to become a boxer in school, climbed mountains, won highest honors as a Harvard student, run a cattle ranch, explored uncharted lands, been elected President of the United States. The year before Indy was born, in 1898, Roosevelt had led a victorious uphill cavalry charge in the Spanish-American War— at age thirty-nine!

"Dad," Indy said, "that's the President you're talking about!"

"*Ex*-president." Professor Jones took a look at Indy's newspaper and read aloud: " 'The esteemed American leader Theodore Roosevelt . . . fearless hunter . . . in charge of an expedition for the Smithsonian Institution to collect animals and plant specimens, especially big game . . .' 'Fearless hunter,' indeed! The man is fifty and out of a job. This is a vacation for him!" He glanced up and saw Indy's puzzled expression. With a weary sigh, he added, "All right, I suppose I am a bit envious of the fellow. Why are you so concerned with him?"

"He's friends with the guy we're visiting, right?"

"Well, yes, but Mr. Medlicot runs a coffee plantation. He doesn't have time to gallivant around with game hunters."

"Too bad." Just what Indy wanted—sitting

around in the African heat and watching coffee beans grow.

"Believe me, it's just as well we won't be crossing Roosevelt's path."

"Why?"

Professor Jones shrugged. "You never know. With his eyesight, he might mistake us for a family of impalas."

"Dad," Indy said innocently, "did anyone ever tell you that you have a strange sense of humor?"

Professor Jones let out a loud belly laugh and tousled Indy's hair. His eyes, though, were focused on something in the distance, behind Indy. "Good lord, signs of civilization!" he said. "I believe we're approaching the Old Port of Mombasa, Junior."

Indy rolled his eyes. "Indiana!" he protested.

"No, British East Africa."

"You know what I mean, Dad," Indy said. "*Call* me Indiana!"

Henry Jones, Junior—that was Indy's real name. But he took his nickname from his dog, Indiana. Why? One, because he loved his dog. Two, because the name sounded great. Simple, right? So why on earth did his dad have to call him *Junior*? The least he could do was call him Henry—or even Jones!

"Sorry, Junior," Professor Jones said with a chuckle. He gave his son a wink, then gazed over the railing.

Indy turned and saw a cluster of buildings on the horizon. "It's about time," he said, and sighed.

"What's the matter? You're bored with our trip?" his dad asked. "Egypt, Paris, and Vienna weren't exciting enough for you?"

"They were great, but they didn't have lions and tigers and—and lechwes!"

As the steamship chugged onward, a bayside city came into view. It was a crowded swirl of colors—boats with billowing sails, carts drawn by horses, buggies drawn by people. There were Europeans wearing crisp, starched linens; Arabs wearing long, flowing caftans; and native tribespeople in well-worn khakis. A huge fortress loomed over the harbor, its stone walls slanting down a tree-covered cliffside.

"Anna! Miss Seymour!" Professor Jones called into the open door of a cabin. "Come look!"

A moment later Mrs. Anna Jones emerged with Indy's private tutor, Helen Seymour. "Oh,

Miss Seymour," Indy's mom said, her eyes lighting up, "isn't it beautiful!"

Mrs. Jones was trim and attractive, with blond hair and soft blue eyes that seemed to know everything. She was as warm as her husband was gruff, yet she shared the same thirst for travel to far-off places.

But Indy barely noticed his mother. Next to her, Helen Seymour looked severely ill. Her jaw was slack and her eyes glazed. Her skin, normally a pale white, was now greenish. Silvergray hair was spilling out of a tight bun in wispy strands.

Indy stared at his tutor in disbelief. She wasn't his favorite person in the world, yet he couldn't help but feel sorry for her right now. Usually she was as tough as they came. She was the kind of person who'd never let weakness show. He'd seen few expressions cross her face other than disapproval or annoyance. *Nausea* made her look almost . . . well, human.

Must have been the chipped beef, Indy realized. Miss Seymour was the only one who'd had it besides him. And, proper Englishwoman that she was, she had finished the whole thing.

He watched Miss Seymour walk to the railing. She managed to keep her back straight, even to force a little smile. For a moment, Indy thought she was feeling better—until the ship suddenly pitched on choppy water. Miss Seymour's smile immediately disappeared.

"Well! A little turbulence, eh, Miss Seymour?" Professor Jones said cheerfully.

Miss Seymour's answer was a small, choked "Urghh . . ." Suddenly she wheeled around and sprinted back into the cabin, her face etched with panic.

Indy tried not to grin. He could forget about lessons, at least for a while. The visit to the British colony was off to a good start.

In Mombasa Professor Jones rented one of the only automobiles in British East Africa—a Model T Ford. After a long, bone-jarring ride over the ruts and thornbushes of a dry, scraggly plain, they arrived at Mr. Medlicot's plantation.

Endless rows of olive-green coffee trees stretched all the way to the horizon. In their midst was a one-story stone house.

As they got closer, Indy saw four men waving and smiling from the house's veranda. Only one of them was a white man, and Indy assumed he was Mr. Medlicot. As the Model T puttered to a stop, the men ran toward it, their feet creating small dust clouds in the parched soil.

Clank! Whozzz! Chuck-a-chuck! The car fought a little before finally dying.

"Welcome, my friends!" Mr. Medlicot said. His eyes shone like flashlights out of his deeply tanned skin. There was a wide smile beneath his bushy mustache as he introduced himself to everyone. The other men, Mr. Medlicot's African servants, took the luggage out of the backseat.

"Medlicot, you old rascal!" Professor Jones said. "You don't look a day older since we read together at Oxford."

"It's this country, Henry!" Medlicot said. "Fresh air, unspoiled land—it's like living in the Garden of Eden!" He led them into the house, then turned to address everyone. "Now, I'm afraid we've not much time. Put your things down and change into some rugged clothes. We're due to leave in a half hour."

"Leave?" Professor Jones said. "We just arrived!"

"Can't turn down an invitation to a safari, can we?" Medlicot went on.

"A *safari*?" Indy repeated.

"How fascinating!" Miss Seymour said. "But

I'm afraid I must impose on your goodwill, Mr. Medlicot, and ask that we leave later—or perhaps tomorrow. You see, I've caught a bit of a stomach sickness . . ."

"Sorry, ma'am, we're all under strict orders to go," Medlicot said. "I've reserved tickets for us on the Nairobi railroad."

"Under strict orders, indeed," Miss Seymour said, her jaw set with determination. "I was under the impression we were guests, not hired hands."

"Of course, ma'am. Staying behind is your prerogative entirely," Medlicot said with a sigh. "Although I'm not exactly sure how I'll explain your absence to Teddy."

"Well, perhaps this 'Teddy' will understand the need to have the common decency to *ask* first," Miss Seymour said.

"Uh, Mr. Medlicot," Indy piped up. "Teddy who?"

Medlicot was at the door, his hand on the knob. Casually he looked over his shoulder and said, "Roosevelt, of course. Now look sharp, the rest of you. I expect you outside in precisely twenty-five minutes or we'll miss the train."

With that, Medlicot left, pulling the door shut behind him.

"Roosevelt . . ." Miss Seymour said under her breath. Her fingers began racing through her hair, tucking in the loose ends. "Well, I never . . . oh, dear . . ."

Indy practically had to scrape his jaw off the floor. He had met a lot of famous people on this trip and done a lot of wild things. But this was different. Now he pictured himself in the sweltering African bush, a rifle at the ready, coming face to face with the most fearsome man-eaters in the world.

And he'd be doing it shoulder to shoulder with the greatest living American hero!

Chapter 2

"Up you go!" Mr. Medlicot said, lifting Indy onto a long, padded seat that was bolted to the front of the train's engine car.

"Thanks," Indy said, even though he didn't really need the boost.

"A bit dangerous, isn't it?" Professor Jones asked. "I mean, what if the seat comes loose while the train's moving?"

"You've grown cautious in your old age, Henry," Medlicot said. "Maybe I should let Miss Seymour take your place. Mrs. Jones practically had to chain her to her seat in the passenger car."

"Yes, well, her stomach, you see . . ." Professor Jones sputtered.

"Teddy had this seat built especially for himself and his party." Mr. Medlicot laughed as he hopped onto the seat himself. "And those chaps are not exactly featherweights. Come along."

As Professor Jones sat down on the other side of Indy, Medlicot signaled over his shoulder to the train's engineer.

With the blast of a horn and a slow, grinding *chug-chug,* the train began to move. It lumbered slowly around the outskirts of Mr. Medlicot's plantation.

As it picked up speed, Indy felt the warm, dry wind against his cheeks. To his left, coffee trees bent in the train's backdraft.

"Yeee-hah!" Indy yelled.

"Keep your eyes open!" Medlicot yelled back. "We're entering the Southern Game Reserve!"

It didn't take long for the game reserve to live up to its name. Ahead of them was a herd of zebras, lazily watching the train approach.

"Look!" Indy shouted.

Phee-oooooo! At the sound of the train's whistle, the zebras began to run. Indy watched in awe as the train caught up and the zebras swerved away. They thundered toward a lush forest at the base of a distant mountain, scattering a flock of large-bodied birds with orange head plumes. In the settling dust, Indy saw a family of gray rodents jumping about like miniature kangaroos.

"Extraordinary!" Professor Jones said. "All this wildlife—and not one sign of human habitation."

Medlicot nodded. "The Garden of Eden!" he shouted proudly.

"Yeah, complete with a railroad!" Indy said.

"Haw!" Medlicot guffawed. "Touché, young man!"

Indy laughed. He felt almost giddy with joy. Across the plain he spotted a herd of gazelles, leaping high into the air. Atop each jump they seemed to hover in the air, as if they were flying.

At that moment, in his heart, Indy felt like one of those gazelles.

An hour later, in an area Medlicot called the Rift Valley, the train stopped at a small station. There, Medlicot rented two horses, one for himself and one for Indy. For the others, he hired an ox-drawn cart and two porters. With

Medlicot in the lead, they rode toward Roosevelt's safari camp.

After another hour, Medlicot pointed to a steep hill ahead. "I believe it's on the other side of that."

Indy couldn't wait. He prodded his horse and raced on ahead.

"Junior! Slow down!" his dad shouted.

Indy pretended not to hear. He charged up the hill—but when he got to the top, he stopped his horse short.

Below him the land sloped downward, then jutted out into a tree-dotted ridge that looked over the endless grasslands. In a large clearing on the ridge were about twenty tents, spread out like a small town. There were several large, thatch-roofed huts with open sides. One of the huts looked like a dining area. Dozens of dark-skinned African tribesmen moved about, dragging animal skins or lugging equipment. Others were cleaning rifles, grooming horses, preparing food. Some of them wore Western-style shirts and pants, but many were bare-chested or dressed in simple, long robes. Near one of the larger tents, a few white men were hotly discussing something.

"Wow . . ." was all Indy could say.

"See those small tents on the right?" came Medlicot's voice behind him.

"Uh-huh," Indy replied.

Medlicot pulled up beside Indy, a mischievous smile on his face. "Last one to them is a skinned wildebeest!"

With a loud "Gee-yahh!" Medlicot charged down the hillside.

"Get him!" Indy cried out, digging his heels into his horse's flanks. In a cloud of dust, the two horses pounded toward the tents as their riders hooted and laughed.

Medlicot won the race by a nose. "Good reflexes, my boy!" he called out.

"Thanks!" Indy said. "Where's President Roosevelt?"

"I'll find out while you unpack," Medlicot answered. "You have first pick of the tents."

Indy tied his horse by one of the tents. Soon his parents and Miss Seymour caught up, and the porters began taking their suitcases off the cart and carrying them to the tents.

Indy ran into his tent with his suitcase and began taking out his clothes and books. Before long Miss Seymour came in. Her face was red and beaded with perspiration. Frowning, she began neatening Indy's things. "Slow down,

Henry," she said. "This wilderness has been here for millions of years. It's not going to disappear while you unpack."

"But I want to see Roosevelt!" Indy said. "He's the best—a president, a boxer, a hunter—"

"And he won't be back till sundown," Miss Seymour cut in.

"How do you know?"

"Your father asked one of the men."

"Okay," Indy said with a sigh of resignation. "I'll slow down."

Miss Seymour shook her head, busily folding clothes. "I feel Mr. Medlicot's boisterous nature is a bad influence on you, Henry."

Indy turned to answer and saw Mr. Medlicot standing in the tent's opening behind Miss Seymour. With a sheepish grin, he said, "Henry, would you like me to show you around the camp before everyone returns?"

"Yes, sir!" Indy practically knocked Miss Seymour over as he sprinted out of the tent.

"Henry!" Miss Seymour called after him. "Just calm down or you'll collapse with sunstroke!"

But Indy was long gone. Mr. Medlicot turned to Miss Seymour and tipped his hat. "Don't worry, ma'am. I'll calm him down."

As he slipped through the open flap, Miss

Seymour raised a wary eyebrow. "Some hope, I'm sure . . ." she said to herself.

Across the camp, Indy was approaching a large tent. From inside came the screeches, whistles, and songs of birds. Tribesmen were taking huge sacks of salt from a pile and moving them into the tent.

"What in the . . ." Indy muttered. He had to look into this.

"Straight through the lungs and spinal cord, just how I like them!" came a voice from inside.

Indy peered into the tent. There were bird cages everywhere—hanging from the roof supports, resting on tables, tucked in the corners. A thin man with glasses walked from cage to cage, making notes in a book.

Indy heard the voice again, coming from his left. "Shame about her cubs, though. Only one of them will be worth exhibiting."

When Indy looked over, his breath caught in his throat. There was a lion on the ground, dead and skinned. Its eyes and mouth were wide open, as if ready to attack. A bearded man— the speaker Indy had heard—was kneeling by the lion's side and examining its head.

Mr. Medlicot strolled into the tent. "Ah,

Heller!" he bellowed. "Let me introduce you to Henry Jones, Junior, Professor Jones's son."

The man stood up. Smiling pleasantly, he extended a hand to Indy.

"Pleased to meet you, Mr. Heller," Indy said. He shook the man's hand, feeling something sticky and warm.

He politely pretended not to notice that his hand was now full of lion blood.

"Heller's one of the taxidermists from the Smithsonian," Mr. Medlicot said. "He's part of Mr. Roosevelt's team. Eventually these lovely creatures will be at the National Museum in Washington—looking much more fearsome than they do now, I assure you."

"Taxidermist?" Indy said. "Does that mean you stuff them?"

"Well, here I just take their measurements, skin them, and preserve the skins in salt so they can be transported back to the States," Mr. Heller said. "The fun starts when I get home. I build a life-size model of the body out of metal, wood, and clay, then I pull the skin over the model and try to make it look alive." Heller gave Indy a crinkly smile. "The next time you go into a museum, you can think of me and my blood-stained hands."

Indy had a much better idea for something

to remember—casually walking into Miss Seymour's tent to start lessons, his hands dripping. If *that* didn't throw her . . .

He quickly put the thought out of his mind. "Uh, you don't happen to have a sink around here, do you?"

Mr. Heller first looked puzzled, then saw Indy's bloody hand. "Oh, yes! We've got water in buckets out back. Feel free."

"Thanks. Excuse me."

As Indy left the tent, he took another glance at the lion. *Someone* had faced those cold eyes, those dagger-like teeth. Someone had held his ground, looking steadily through a rifle's sights, as the beast attacked. Indy shivered. What a feeling that must be! Absolutely terrifying.

He couldn't wait to try it someday.

Out back, he washed his hands while looking over the ridge. The sun was setting over the grasslands, casting a dusky orange-brown light. Strangely, the vista reminded Indy of the ocean, spreading out to the horizon in all directions.

His eyes stopped at the sight of some small, dark huts in the distance. There was thick brush all around them, like a barricade. Inside the compound Indy could spot the movement of a couple of large animals.

Indy looked back over his shoulder. He could

hear Mr. Medlicot, still in the taxidermists' tent. His parents were nowhere to be seen, and he caught a glimpse of Miss Seymour fussing about her tent.

They wouldn't miss him. Not for the time it would take to go and look at the strange little village. After all, why should he have to hang around and wait? It wasn't *his* fault that he had unpacked faster than anyone. It wasn't *his* fault that Roosevelt wasn't back yet.

There had to be a place where he could climb down safely. Indy scampered to the edge of the ridge and peered over.

The last thing he expected to see was someone peering back.

Below him, surrounded by four quietly grazing goats, was a young native boy about Indy's age. He was standing on one leg, holding onto a long wooden walking stick for support. His eyes had the stillness of a person who had seen everything and refused to be surprised.

The two boys held their stares. The native boy's face showed neither friendship nor hostility. Indy wanted to say something, but wasn't sure what.

Miss Seymour's voice pierced the silence. "Henry! *Henry!* They're back!"

Indy's heart jumped with excitement. The strange, still-faced boy would have to wait. President Roosevelt and his hunting party had returned to camp—and Indy wanted to be there to meet them.

Chapter 3

Indy's feet pounded the hard, dusty earth. Across the camp, everyone had gathered near a cluster of bushes and trees. One by one, dirt-smeared hunters emerged from the bushes, to a chorus of cheers.

"Henry! Over here!" Medlicot shouted, waving from the crowd.

Next to him stood Indy's parents and Miss Seymour. They were chatting with one of the hunters, an older man with a white beard and leathery, sun-browned skin.

Mr. Medlicot gestured to the older man as

Indy approached. "Henry, this is Frederick Selous," he said, pronouncing the last name "Say-LOO." "He helped plan the safari and is one of the best hunters in all of Africa."

Smiling, Mr. Selous shook Indy's hand. "Good to meet you, Henry."

"It's good to be here," Indy replied.

To their left, a thin young man struggled with a tripod and camera. "Mr. Selous," the man called out, "can you give me a hand before Father gets here?"

"Certainly, Kermit," Selous called to the man. Turning to Medlicot, he said, "Excuse me."

As Selous walked away, Medlicot remarked to Indy, "Kermit is Roosevelt's son. Twenty years old. His father pulled him out of Harvard to go on this safari."

Kermit hurriedly spread out the spindly legs of a tripod, which held a boxy camera. A thick piece of cloth hung over the top and back of the camera, and Kermit ducked under it. Looking through the lens, he aimed the camera at the bushes. Then he reached into a carrying case, took out a metal container on a stick, and filled it with flash powder. As he handed the stick to Mr. Selous, a thunderous voice boomed from behind the bushes:

"Kermit! Are you ready?"

With a nervous jump, Kermit got behind the camera. "Yes, Dad, all set!" he called back. "Come on in!"

Indy trained his eyes on the thick bush. Its dusty green leaves were now glowing red in the fiery light of the sunset. The entire camp had fallen silent.

There was a clopping of hooves. A horse emerged, tall and muscular. On it was a man, short and squat. He had squinty eyes, thick glasses, a potbelly, and a smile that seemed to show every one of his enormous teeth.

And yet Indiana Jones had never seen anyone so magnetic.

He couldn't help but stare. Roosevelt's face was like a stone sculpture, powerful and deeply etched. His shoulders were broad, his chest like a sturdy rain barrel. And his eyes radiated both intelligence and kindness. Theodore Roosevelt looked like a man with no fear, a man who never, *ever* doubted himself.

And from the looks on the faces around the camp, no one else doubted him either.

With a loud *pooof!* the flash powder exploded, drenching Roosevelt and his horse in lightning-white light.

"Oh, bully!" Roosevelt said with a chuckle,

blinking his eyes exaggeratedly. "*You* were ready, but I wasn't."

The whole crowd burst out laughing. Every eye was turned to him, every face smiling.

"Sorry, Dad," Kermit said, reaching up to help Roosevelt off the horse. "I hope I didn't blind you."

"Perfectly all right," Roosevelt said as he stepped down. "I was already blind with hunger. Have our guests arrived?"

"They're here," Kermit said. "These are Professor and Mrs. Jones; Henry, Junior; and young Henry's tutor, Helga Seymour."

"Helen," Miss Seymour politely corrected him.

"Dee-*lighted*!" Roosevelt's voice was almost an enthusiastic bark. He shook everyone's hand, then said, "Pleased to meet you all, and you'll excuse me for saying I am absolutely ravenous! Professor, I would be honored if your family would join us for some fresh roasted game. And by saying 'family,' I naturally mean to include you, Miss Seaford."

Miss Seymour did something Indy had never seen her do before. She blushed. Then, to Indy's complete astonishment, she smiled and said, "The honor would be mine indeed, Mr. President."

"Splendid." Roosevelt looked at his wristwatch and said, "I shall clean up, and then we can proceed to dinner."

With that, he headed to a large tent with an American flag flying beside it. Indy looked at Miss Seymour. She was fiddling with her hair again, and her eyes were darting toward Roosevelt. "You didn't correct him," Indy said. "He called you Miss *Seaford.*"

Miss Seymour looked at Indy suddenly, as if snapping out of a dream. "He did?" she said. "I . . . I didn't notice."

She went on to her tent, businesslike as ever. Indy wanted to say something, but kept his mouth shut. For a brief moment, he had seen a new side of Miss Seymour—a shy, uncertain side. And he kind of liked it.

That night the entire camp was ablaze with campfires. Roosevelt's party ate dinner in the open-sided dining hut at a table set with a linen cloth and china plates and wine glasses. Indy was disgusted to find out that he had to wear a suit and tie. He'd looked forward to roughing it on safari. But Roosevelt didn't seem to mind dressing up, so Indy kept his complaints to himself.

Around the dinner table, conversation was fast and loud. Indy found out a lot of things he hadn't known. Roosevelt explained that the camp was in a place called the Kapiti Plains, south of Nairobi. That the native workers were mostly Swahili, who lived on the East African coast. That they were the backbone of the safari and were divided into five different groups: porters, to carry the killed animals; *askaris,* or soldiers; *saises,* in charge of the horses; tent handlers; and gun bearers.

But Indy enjoyed the hunting stories best of all. Roosevelt seemed to remember the details of every animal he had killed. "As you can see," he said, "we're at the end of the dry season, and the condition of the land bears witness. On the plain there's practically no cover whatsoever, except for euphorbias and a few stunted mimosas. Nonetheless, Kermit and I bagged some Tommies and Grants today."

"Who?" Indy said, his mouth full of some unidentified but tasty meat.

"Thomson's gazelles and Grant's gazelles," Kermit explained. "A lot of the animals are named after the first Europeans who saw them."

"Mm-hm," Indy replied, chomping on another savory forkful.

Roosevelt gave Indy a broad smile. "Cooked to your taste, Henry?"

"Rrrurgghl" was the closest Indy could get to "Exactly."

"Henry," Mrs. Jones said in her best scolding voice.

"The boy's got a man's appetite," Roosevelt said with a laugh. "Enjoy it, young fellow. It was a stout-hearted beast. You should have seen the fight it put up."

Indy almost gagged. "You mean, this was today's . . . catch?"

"Couldn't be fresher," Roosevelt said proudly. "And it was one of the plumper wildebeest cows we've seen in a while!"

Wildebeest?

Indy took a few more chews and swallowed. Suddenly the meat seemed a little tough, a little stringy. Somehow, when he didn't *know* what he was eating, it had tasted pretty good.

He looked up to see Roosevelt smiling proudly at him. Indy turned his lips upward in return, then bravely dug his fork in again.

"I understand you brought quite a library with you," Mrs. Jones said brightly, changing the subject.

"As important as a good rifle collection, and much more entertaining," Roosevelt said. "Feel free to use it—I have Shakespeare, Homer, Shelley, Longfellow, Poe, Euripides, Dickens . . ." He looked at Indy. "Also Bret Harte and Mark Twain. I did not, however, bring Professor Henry Jones's book on medieval armor—but only because I finished it before I left. And I thought it was a fine work."

Indy's dad beamed. "Thank you, sir, I'm glad you enjoyed it. It sounds as if you read a lot."

"Not as much as I'd like to," Roosevelt replied. "I can only manage a couple of books a day here. Medlicot says your lecture tour is related to a newer publication, though?"

"Two publications, actually," Professor Jones said. "One on the medieval chivalric code and another on the Holy Grail . . ."

Professor Jones's voice was drowned out by a loud exchange between Kermit, Heller, Medlicot, and Selous.

"How peculiar," Selous was saying, looking at a page in a large leather-bound book called *African Mammals.*

"Every herd of antelope we've seen has turned

out to be beisas or gemsboks," Kermit added. "Look at this, Dad," he said, passing the book to his father.

"Excuse me," Roosevelt said to Professor Jones. He peered at the open page, which had a map and several drawings of horned animals.

"You see, sir," Heller said, pointing to one of the animals, "they clearly indicate this as being one of the breeding grounds for the fringe-eared oryx. It's a type of antelope. There should be thousands of them here."

Indy looked at the picture of the oryx. The first thing he noticed was its long, tapered horns. Like two ridged spears, they jutted straight back, in line with the slant of the snout. The animal's body had the graceful legs and hindquarters of a horse and the stout chest of a bull. Black stripes, like paintstrokes, ran along its rib cage, separating its fawn-colored upper body from its white belly. There were more stripes on the head and a black band around each thigh. Atop each ear was a small tassel of black hair.

"I haven't seen any this year," Selous said.

Roosevelt squinted through his thick glasses. "Hmm . . . that's quite a mystery, then."

"Mind you, this was written twenty years ago," said Heller.

"They can't have just died out," Roosevelt said.

"It's possible they migrated north," Selous suggested. "They favor dry areas."

Indy's mom was now looking at the book. "What a beautiful animal," she said.

"It's a rare breed," said Roosevelt. "There have been problems tracking it down."

Grrrrrrr . . .

All sound stopped—every voice, every stirring of small animals, every insect noise.

There was a rustling in a thicket. Indy figured it came from fifty yards away.

Rrrr . . . Rrrr!

Something was lurking in the pitch darkness of the moonless night. Something that was very large and very unhappy.

Around the campfires, tribesmen rose to their feet. Some of them grabbed spears.

"That would be a lion, I suppose," Miss Seymour said, trying to sound calm.

Roosevelt's eyes were staring out into the blackness, as if he were trying to burn a hole into it. His only answer to Miss Seymour was a small, tense nod.

Chapter 4

Grrrrrrr . . .

Indy became aware of movement all around the dining hut. At each campfire, the tribesmen were turning in the direction of the lion. One of them began a soft, rhythmic chant.

The others joined in, one by one. The chant grew into a low, mysterious song. The dry nighttime air seemed to sharpen the sound, make every voice stand out.

Miss Seymour forced a smile. "Well, at least we're in safe company."

"No hunter is safe, Miss Seymour," Selous replied, his voice nearly a whisper. "Today I shot a lioness whose mate was nearby—"

"I tried to kill the mate," Roosevelt added, "but unfortunately I only wounded it. We must never underestimate a wounded lion. I can tell you of a hunter who learned that the hard way. . . . Remember, Selous?"

A flicker of a smile crossed Selous's face. "Teddy, you don't believe that old story, do you?"

"Believe it? I was there! The man had shot the lion, but he failed to finish it off, and it limped away. Well, the poor fellow was scared out of his wits. He even built a tree house to sleep in, thinking he'd be safe, but the wounded beast came into the camp that night and smelled him out! There was nothing we could do. . . ."

Grrrrrrrr . . .

The growling sounded much closer. The tribesmen's song now grew into a loud babble of voices, with sudden small shouts. Selous picked up a rifle and checked to see that it was loaded, then went outside.

Indy felt the hair rising on the back of his neck. His muscles tensed and his heart raced.

If the lion attacked, it would be fast. There would be only one chance to stop it.

Roosevelt glanced at Indy and said, "Do you know how to shoot a gun, Henry?"

"No, sir," Indy admitted.

"He's only ten years old," Mrs. Jones protested.

"By the time *I* was ten, I had an intimate knowledge of firearms," Roosevelt replied. He gave Indy a confident smile. "Tomorrow, my boy, I will teach you how to shoot!"

Anna Jones cast a wary look at her husband, but he just gave her a shrug and a nod. *How can you say no to a president*? he seemed to be saying.

Suddenly Indy forgot about the lion. As far as he was concerned, there could be a pride of lions lurking around them. Or a pack of dinosaurs. Who cared? Tomorrow, the most famous hunter in America was going to teach him to use a gun!

The growling stopped an hour or so later. Warily the camp settled into sleep, with a double shift of askaris rotating throughout the rest of the night.

The next morning, after a breakfast of fried

leftover wildebeest, Indy got his shooting lesson.

A large watermelon from the supply tent was the target. Roosevelt set it in the outskirts of camp, paced out about fifty yards, and gave Indy one of his shotguns. "A Fox Number Twelve shotgun," he said with pride. "No better gun was ever made."

Indy ran his hand along its worn wooden stock. The gun was heavier than he had expected.

"All right, Henry, take aim," Roosevelt said.

That was it? *Take aim?* For a second, Indy wanted to ask for more instructions. But the urge quickly passed. When someone like Roosevelt told you to take aim, you took aim.

He brought the gun to his shoulder. Carefully he lined up the melon in its sight.

"Now, squeeze the trigger," Roosevelt said. "Don't pull it. Squeeze it."

Indy gritted his teeth. He squeezed.

Blammm!

As he jerked back from the recoil of the shotgun, one end of the watermelon exploded. Hunks of green rind and red pulp burst outward and fell to the ground.

"Well done," Roosevelt said. "Now, again."

Indy fired once more. The melon jumped and erupted.

Roosevelt nodded toward the gun. "Now break it," he demanded.

Indy gave him a puzzled look. "But . . . but don't you need it?" he said.

"No, no, I'll show you." Roosevelt grabbed the shotgun and thrust it down over his knee. It opened on a hinge at the end of the barrels, sending the empty shells onto the ground. Then he loaded two more shells, snapped the gun together, and said, "Now try again."

Indy got off a few more shots, and soon the melon was reduced to a small shapeless mass. Out of the corner of his eye, he could see Roosevelt nodding with approval.

"Good boy! I can see you are going to be quite a marksman," Roosevelt said. Then, taking the gun from Indy, he added, "Always remember, a gun should only be used in order to survive."

"Father!" came Kermit's voice from behind them. "We're leaving!"

Roosevelt looked over his shoulder. Kermit, Selous, Professor Jones, Medlicot, and several askaris and porters were on their horses, ready for the day's hunt. "See you later, Junior!" Professor Jones called out.

"Looks like it's time to go," Roosevelt said.

As he mounted his horse, Miss Seymour emerged from her tent with an armful of books. Spotting Indy, she began walking toward him.

Indy's heart sank. If he could only have a *choice* between lessons and hunting . . .

Roosevelt seemed to read his mind. "You may not be able to come out on the hunt with us, but you should at least be able to observe this fine land." With a broad smile, he took the binoculars from around his neck and handed them down to Indy. "Keep them. They're yours!"

"Thank you, sir!" Indy said.

"You look after him now, Miss Seymour," Roosevelt called out. Then, giving Indy a stern look, he added, "And you be good!"

Indy couldn't wipe the grin off his face. "Yes sir, I will!"

Roosevelt gave his horse a swift kick and began trotting off with the other hunters.

Indy watched for a few moments as the hunters grew smaller in the light of the early morning. He had completely forgotten about Miss Seymour until he heard her sigh.

"Wouldn't you like to go hunting, Miss Seymour?" he asked.

She nodded wistfully. "I daresay I would. Especially if I had been invited by someone as dashing and brave as Mr. Roosevelt."

Indy raised an eyebrow. Miss Seymour was trying to make her comment sound polite and proper, but Indy knew better. He recognized a crush when he saw one. "I daresay you would," he said.

Miss Seymour raised her eyebrow. Clearing her throat, she said, "But we have an interesting day ahead of us, Henry. Mr. Heller has lent us some of his zoology books."

They went across the camp. Miss Seymour set the books down on a small wooden desk in front of Indy's tent and pulled up two chairs.

First she insisted on giving Indy two of his regular lessons in history and math. But after lunch she turned to Mr. Heller's books.

Indy glanced at the title of the book on top: *African Mammals*. He remembered Mr. Heller showing the book to President Roosevelt— something about a missing antelope . . .

Indy began flipping through the book, looking for the section on antelopes. He tried to think of the name of the mysterious animal.

"Now, if you'll open that to page—" Miss Seymour began.

But Indy was too absorbed to hear her.

" 'From the giant eland,' " he began reading aloud, " 'weighing up to a ton and standing six feet high, to the smallest, the royal antelope, measuring only ten inches . . .' Wow."

Miss Seymour tried again. "Where do you think the word *antelope* comes from, Henry?"

"Uh . . . *antholops* . . ." Indy said distractedly. "It means 'brightness of eye.' At least that's what it says here. 'There are more than eighty species . . .' "

"And they're hunted by lions and leopards and nearly a dozen other predators, including man . . ." said Miss Seymour, reading over Indy's shoulder.

"The fringe-eared oryx! That's what it was!" Indy blurted out as he found the drawing. It was like no other animal he'd ever seen. It was as powerful-looking as an ox, yet somehow delicate and graceful. "Wow . . . it's beautiful."

"Mm, it certainly is," Miss Seymour said. Again she tried to continue the lesson, but Indy's mind was on the oryx. Were there any around? What could have happened to them? Roosevelt would be *amazed* if Indy could find the answers.

Indy reached under the table for his journal,

a book of blank pages his dad had given him in Egypt. In it, he had been recording his thoughts and observations about his trip. Looking at the picture of the oryx, he began copying it as best he could.

"Why are you putting that in your notebook?" Miss Seymour asked.

"I'm going to take my binoculars and look for it. I'm going to find it for the President and the Smithsonian." Done with his drawing, Indy closed the notebook and held it tightly. "This way, I'll know for sure if I see it."

Miss Seymour smiled and gave up on the lesson. "Very well, but stay near the camp."

Indy put the binoculars around his neck. "I will."

He left his tent and ran across the camp. From the number of animals being dragged to Mr. Heller's tent and the loudness of the screeching birds, Indy could tell the taxidermists had a lot to do. His mother was inside the tent too, helping them organize their records and make labels. No one seemed to notice him as he headed straight for the ridge's edge.

He stopped at the same spot where he'd been the day before. Sitting down, he lifted his binoculars and looked toward the distant village.

He had to cup his hand over the lens to shade out the glare of the afternoon sun.

Indy could now see the native village clearly. There were nearly twenty mud huts, all small and oval-shaped. From this distance they looked like a nest of giant eggs left to incubate in the sun. Two of the huts in the center were much larger than the others. The entire village was within a thorny fence, and Indy could see tribespeople dressed in simple, flowing robes. There seemed to be an awful lot of cattle, too, roaming around freely with the people.

"Beeaaaahh!"

Indy dropped his binoculars at the sound of a high-pitched bleat. He looked down to see a goat running toward the ridge. Behind it stood the dark-skinned boy. He was still with the other goats, still standing on one leg, as if he hadn't moved since the day before.

Indy quickly climbed down the ridge and stood in the way of the wandering goat. With a gentle shooing motion, he got it to turn back to the boy.

Once again, the two of them stared at each other blankly. But this time Indy was determined to make contact.

"Hello," he tried.

The boy shifted to the other leg. He answered Indy with a rapid-fire sentence, in a language that bore no relationship to anything Indy had ever heard.

"I'm sorry, I . . . don't understand," Indy said slowly. Pointing to himself, he said, "Indy . . . my name is Indy. . . ."

He pointed to the other boy. With a sudden jerk, the boy moved away, as if Indy's finger were a loaded gun.

Bad move, Indy realized. Pointing a finger was probably some kind of bad-luck sign. Maybe even a dirty gesture. Suddenly Indy felt self-conscious. What if head-nodding was taboo? Or clearing your throat?

"In . . . dee," the boy said.

It was working! Indy smiled. He reached out to shake the boy's hand, but the boy moved back.

Oops.

"Meto!" a distant voice shouted. *Meto!*

Two young men were running toward them from the small village. They shouted something else to the boy, and he shouted back.

Indy guessed they were telling the boy to come home, because he began moving his goats in their direction.

"Meto?" Indy said. "Is that your name? Meto?"

The boy looked surprised for a moment. Then, for the first time, he returned Indy's smile.

Indy tried to think of something meaningful to say, but "Hi" was all that came out.

Meto nodded, then began walking away.

Oh, great, Indy thought. Just when we were getting somewhere, he has to go.

His promise to Miss Seymour echoed in his head. As much as he wanted to chase after Meto, he had said he wouldn't go too far.

With a frustrated sigh, he watched Meto walking off. The boy had covered a decent amount of ground already. Indy figured he'd reach the village in fifteen minutes or so. And who knew if he'd ever come back?

Fifteen minutes.

That was about how long it took to walk to the grocery store in Indy's hometown of Princeton, New Jersey. Or to the university, where his dad worked. And those were in the neighborhood.

Still, Princeton wasn't British East Africa. Who knew what this tribe was like? Who knew what they thought of curious white intruders?

Indy looked back at the camp. Then, holding onto his binoculars, he decided what he had to do.

He began to walk. Toward the village.

46

Chapter 5

Meto stopped. Even without looking, he knew he was being followed. He turned to face Indy, leveling a hard stare at him. When Meto spoke, there was no mistaking the angry tone of his voice. The words flew out of his mouth in a torrent—guttural, yet somehow smooth and musical.

Indy thought quickly. Taking the binoculars from around his neck, he held them out to Meto. "Binoculars," he said. "Field glasses."

Meto stood silently. Indy moved closer, raising the binoculars up to his own eyes. "You know what these are for? Here, I'll show you."

Indy looked through them and got the village in clear focus. Then he held them up so Meto could look through.

Meto hesitated. Cautiously he moved closer to peer through the lenses.

One glance was all it took. Meto grabbed the binoculars and began looking all around, his mouth open with wonder.

"Look," Indy said, "you can do this, too." He took the binoculars and looked through the large side of the lenses, then gave them to Meto again.

Meto howled with laughter when he saw the tiny image.

Indy felt relief rushing through him. He couldn't help but laugh himself. "Theodore Roosevelt gave them to me," he began to explain.

But Meto cut him off with an excited barrage of words. He took Indy by the arm and began leading him toward the village.

From a distance, the thorn fence had looked kind of scraggly. But as they approached, Indy saw it was at least six feet high, and almost as thick. Any attacker (or cow) that tried to get through would be ripped to shreds.

A couple of young men were waiting by the opening. Eying Indy warily, they herded Meto's goats inside. Meto followed them, gesturing for Indy to wait.

Indy peered inside. The huts were much smaller than he expected, like tiny bunkers. Children ran among them, laughing and shouting. Beyond the children, women sat outside, making clothing and preparing food.

But Indy's attention was captured by a group of men standing beside one of the larger huts. They wore leather bands around their heads, gold bracelets up their arms, and colorful beaded necklaces. Each of them had a spear slung over his back.

When one of them caught a glance of Indy, he clutched his spear and shouted something. Indy had no idea what it meant, but he felt reasonably sure it wasn't "Howdy."

Before Indy could answer, Meto ran out with two small, sharp sticks. Giving one to Indy, he pantomimed a spearing motion, then gestured for Indy to follow him.

The two boys began running away from the village, into the open plain. Indy couldn't believe how fast Meto moved. He seemed to glide, his bare feet hardly touching the ground.

Indy had to sprint to keep up. He half expected Meto to take him all the way to Mombasa. They seemed to run for miles. By the time Meto stopped at the top of a ridge, Indy's lungs felt as if they were going to explode.

Meto crouched behind some thorny bushes. He poked the binoculars between the branches and looked through. Panting, Indy pulled up behind him. He knelt down and tried to take the glasses, but Meto held onto them. Indy pushed aside some branches and gazed out over the plain.

A gasp caught in his throat. It was one of the most spectacular views he had ever seen. Laid out like a great silvery mirror was a vast water hole, surrounded by trees and grass and masses of wild animals.

Zebras, gazelles, and buffalo sipped lazily. From Mr. Heller's book Indy recognized a group of wildebeests, huge and stocky like American bison, but with strangely flat and narrow faces. Hundreds of birds moved around the large animals. And what birds! Tiny multicolored ones flitted around solid turkey-like three-footers; small birds with proud fiery-red combs walked among larger birds with quizzical pointy heads.

At last Meto handed Indy the binoculars, and

he treated himself to a long look. After studying the water hole, he slowly swept the binoculars around to his left. He could pick out small creatures hiding in the nearby brush, then a sudden skittering motion from a clump of trees. He twisted around some more, squinting, trying to see what was among the trees . . .

. . . until all that was in view was a pair of fierce, narrow eyes, coming closer and closer.

Indy's blood ran cold. He had read about lions, even seen them in zoos. But he'd never come face to face with one in the wild.

"Uh . . . lion," Indy whispered. "King . . . boss . . . big cat . . ." He got up to run.

Instantly Meto yanked him back to the ground. Then, with a whispered warning, Meto began pulling Indy away from the ridge. They walked backward on tiptoe, keeping close to the bushes.

Indy heard the violent thumping of tribal drums, muffled but somehow quite close. He thought of the warriors in Meto's village. A posse, he said to himself. This ought to be fun.

It took about two seconds for him to realize that the drums were the sound of his own heart—and he and Meto might just wind up being supper.

All at once Meto stopped short. Indy froze.

There was a soft rustling in the bushes. Wide-eyed, the two boys watched as the lion emerged above them. With its gaze focused on the water hole, it padded gently along the ridgetop—and right into the spot Indy and Meto had left.

Slowly the lion worked its way over the ridge and out of sight. Indy crept forward until he could see the water hole again.

The animals were still there, drinking, chattering, lazy in the afternoon sun. None of them saw the lion approaching through the brush. None of them saw it crouch behind a bush, its muscles taut as a statue's.

But they all saw it pounce.

In an instant everything changed. Birds screeched, zebras reared up, buffalo lowered their horns.

The lion flashed its teeth, lunging at a wildebeest. It tore into the wildebeest with all its might, forcing the creature to the ground.

Indy winced. "Easy, fella," he muttered. "It doesn't taste *that* good."

Out of the corner of his eye, he spotted Meto walking toward a nearby hill. Wasting no time, he followed. The frightening bellows and squawks soon faded in the distance.

They went along another part of the ridge,

then up a hill. There, near a gnarly, flat-topped tree, Meto reached into a pouch around his waist. He pulled out a flute.

Sitting against the tree, Meto played a soft melody. Then he handed Indy the flute. Indy tried to copy him—and sounded awful. Meto laughed and showed Indy some fingerings. Indy played again, getting one or two notes right.

They both smiled. At last they were finding a common language.

In the distance, a flock of enormous birds took off from the plain. As Indy watched them fly across the swollen orange sun, he bolted to his feet. "I have to get back!" he blurted out.

Meto seemed to know what Indy meant. He nodded and started to walk down the hill.

Together, he and Indy made their way across the plain, stepping around occasional bushes and trees. They were silent, and Indy noticed a strange, worried expression on Meto's face.

"What is it?" he asked.

That was when he heard a low rumbling noise. The ground started to vibrate, and Indy thought an earthquake had started. But Meto was looking into the distance, where a cloud of dust was rising upward, cresting just below the circle of the sun.

Indy's eyes widened. "Holy smokes!" he said. It was a stampede! It stretched left and right for what seemed to be miles—and it was gaining on them faster than he thought possible. Running away was out of the question. They'd never get far enough.

"Meto!" Indy shouted. "What do we do?"

Meto didn't reply. His eyes were glued to the herd, as if he were going to stand there and wait.

By now Indy could see the powerful shoulders of the animals, the weird flatness of their faces, the curve of their menacing horns.

Wildebeests, Indy realized. What a twist. He was about to be gored by the same animal he'd eaten for breakfast!

Arriving at Roosevelt's safari camp on the Kapiti Plains.

Roosevelt entertains his guests at dinner with chilling tales of big-game hunting.

Indy (in white pith helmet) visits the Maasai kraal.

Indy gets his first shooting lesson from an old pro.

(Above) Miss Seymour tries to give Indy his lesson,
but he'd rather be drawing the fringe-eared oryx.

(Below) Indy asks Meto to help him track down the fringe-eared oryx.

(Above) The Maasai take Indy to meet the Laibon.

(Left) Hot on the trail, Indy and Meto unearth a root melon.

(Above) The fringe-eared oryx, at last.

(Above) Indy grabs Roosevelt's gun . . . just in time to save a few oryxes.

(Below) As a good-bye gift, Indy gives Meto his prized binoculars.

Chapter 6

Indy stiffened, hypnotized by the approaching horde. He was barely aware of Meto's hand closing around his shoulder.

The next thing he knew, Meto was dragging him toward a large fallen tree. There, behind its thick trunk, they huddled tight.

The stampeding herd came closer and closer. Indy hugged the ground. Suddenly the wildebeests were leaping over the tree trunk, over his head, hundreds and hundreds of them. They sprayed the boys with dirt, and Indy shut his eyes tightly. The shaking earth jarred his teeth, the hooves thundered so loud his ears ached. The smell was overpowering.

And then, like a passing freight train, the noise receded. The rumbling faded, then stopped. There was a muffled silence. Indy opened his eyes.

He looked over at Meto and was met by a broad grin and a shrug. Then, as if on cue, they both exploded with laughter, whooping at the top of their lungs.

A few hundred yards away, the wildebeests were slowing down, wading across a river. Indy watched them in awe, full of admiration for the creatures that had almost killed him.

Meto began chattering away. "Whoa . . . whoa . . ." Indy said. Then he remembered a phrase in Meto's language. It was something Meto had said on the ridge when Indy got up to run from the approaching lion. Indy figured it must have meant "Take it easy" or "Slow down." He repeated it.

Meto did a double take. Then he smiled and slowly looked around. Pointing to a blade of grass, he said a word. Indy repeated it. *Tree, sky, earth*—one by one, Indy and Meto exchanged words from each other's language as they walked back toward Roosevelt's camp.

Indy had escaped death with Meto, and now he felt he'd found a friend for life.

Once again, Indy made it back to camp just as the hunters were returning. And once again, no one seemed to notice he'd been gone.

He strolled up to the crowd, which was gathered in front of Roosevelt, Kermit, and Selous. The hunters were smiling proudly, next to two severed rhinoceros heads on the ground. Professor Jones and Medlicot were manning the camera. When the flash went off, everyone cheered.

Indy rushed toward Roosevelt, but he wasn't the first to get there. Miss Seymour was.

"What extraordinary specimens," she said, looking at the two heads.

"It took quite a time to get the big one," Roosevelt said proudly. "She charged me and I felled her at a distance of thirty yards. I think she intended mischief."

Indy stared at the two rhinos with amazement. The heads themselves each looked about as heavy as Indy himself. Their horns looked strong enough to pierce steel. "Were you scared?" he asked.

Roosevelt knelt down next to Indy. "Nope, excited," he said. "These animals are very rare. Now, with these two, that makes seven we've managed to bag so far."

"But if they're so rare, why do you kill so many of them?" Indy asked.

Mr. Selous answered that one. "In the grand scheme of things, seven is not that many, my boy. There are many thousands of them."

"Beasts such as these belong in a museum," Roosevelt insisted, "for everyone to share."

"Besides," Mr. Selous added, "it's a wonderful sport."

With a satisfied nod, Roosevelt picked up his gun and began to walk away.

Indy followed close behind. Somehow, Roosevelt's statements weren't making sense. "Trigger-happy" was what the professor had called Roosevelt, back on the steamship. Indy had figured his dad was just trying to be funny. Now he wasn't so sure. "But it still doesn't seem right to me," Indy said.

"You're missing the point, Henry," Roosevelt said. "This is for science. If people are educated, they'll have more respect for wildlife and nature."

"Then why not shoot one or two?" Indy asked.

"Because there are *hundreds* of museums." Roosevelt looked and sounded impatient, but Indy still wasn't satisfied with the explanation.

"But couldn't you put one different kind of animal in each museum?"

Roosevelt exploded. *"It is very important that mankind come to understand nature!"*

Indy backed away. He hadn't expected Roosevelt to shout at him like that.

Obviously, neither had Roosevelt. His angry expression melted away. With a sigh, he stood up and began packing his gun into its case. "Look, I understand your feelings, son. Why, I was given this very gun in recognition of my efforts to preserve a natural heritage. I count few achievements higher than the founding of five national parks, where people can come to understand and respect nature."

"Oh," Indy said. "I . . . guess I see."

Roosevelt began strolling toward the edge of the ridge. Around him the tribesmen were fanning campfires into life. Indy followed behind Roosevelt, trying to sort out his explanation: Kill the animals. Stuff them and display them. Put them in museums so people can study them. Then set up wildlife parks, where people can appreciate the living animals. It made sense . . . kind of.

But Indy was still confused. He figured there must be some reason the rare animals were rare. Maybe they were diseased; maybe they didn't have enough of the right food. But if Roosevelt was hunting them for museums, how could that possibly help them?

And what about the animals whose homes were *not* in parks? Should everyone be allowed to hunt them?

"You see, Henry, knowledge is the key," Roosevelt said, pausing to look over the grassland. "Mankind has the power to destroy the wilderness, and that is something we must never be allowed to do."

In the dying sunlight, Indy could see puffs of smoke arising from Meto's village. He thought about the afternoon, about the trip to the water hole, about Meto's knowledge of the animals of the plain.

Then a thought came to him. If anyone could help him find the fringe-eared oryx, Meto could.

Indy figured he'd broach the subject carefully. "Mr. Roosevelt, do you know anything about that place?" Indy said, pointing to the village.

Roosevelt nodded. "Maasai people live there. They're very peaceful. Herders by nature. They practically worship cattle. I believe their village is called a kraal."

"Do you know their language?" Indy asked.

"The Maa language is very tough," Roosevelt replied. "For the life of me, I haven't been able to get a handle on it. Why do you ask?"

"Oh . . . I've, uh, read that they can track animals really well. I was thinking—"

"Checkers, old man?" Roosevelt suddenly asked.

Indy's eyes lit up. Checkers was his favorite game. "Sure!"

They went to the dining hut, where Roosevelt got a checkerboard and pieces as well as a kerosene lantern. Outside, they set up the game by a campfire and began playing.

Within a few minutes, Indy had cleared most of Roosevelt's pieces. He couldn't help grinning.

"Well, well . . ." Roosevelt said, raising an eyebrow.

Indy felt flushed with pride. Confidently,

he decided to bring up his idea. "What do you think happened to the fringe-eared oryx, Mr. Roosevelt?"

"I don't know," Roosevelt said. "It's a mystery."

"I've been thinking about it."

"You have?"

"Yes, sir, and I think I can help."

"Well, the Smithsonian needs that animal for its collection. I'd like to be able to oblige them."

"In fact," Indy said, "I *know* I can find it."

A smile spread across Roosevelt's face. "Good, so I can depend on you, eh?"

He's humoring me, Indy thought. He thinks I'm just a show-off. Well, he'll see.

With a self-assured nod, Indy said, "Yes, Mr. Roosevelt. I promise."

Crracck! Crracck!

Roosevelt and Indy spun around at the sound of two gunshots. They jumped to their feet and ran toward it.

At the edge of camp, Mr. Selous stood with a smoldering rifle. He stared into the distant blackness.

As Indy and Roosevelt joined him, there was a chorus of happy shouting from the brush.

Tribesmen were now gathering around the clearing, some of them singing.

Indy heard a steady, rhythmic cracking of branches. A group of porters came into the dim light of the camp, straining to carry a huge stretcher—a stretcher that barely held the body of a dead lion.

A loud cheer went up from all around. Indy threw back his head and yelled, "Yeee-hah!"

The lion had come back, looking to settle its score with Mr. Selous and President Roosevelt —just like the lion in Roosevelt's story! Indy wondered what would have happened if Mr. Selous hadn't heard it lurking in the brush.

And from the ash-gray look on Selous's face, he must have been wondering the same thing.

Chapter 7

Indy laid his notebook open on the ground in front of Meto. He felt a little funny, having sneaked away to the kraal so early in the morning. Only Miss Seymour had seen him, but she'd barely said good morning. She seemed occupied with fixing her hair and smiling into the mirror—things he'd *never* seen her do before she met President Roosevelt.

But right now, Indy could only afford to think of his mission. He was determined to find the oryx before anyone at camp knew he was missing.

The morning sun, rising swiftly above the horizon, lit up the notebook page. In the kraal, Maasai children were beginning to run out of their huts, shouting happily to each other.

"Oryx," Indy said.

Meto crouched low, resting his walking stick on the ground. He stared at the drawing, then said a word in Maa.

Indy repeated the word.

Meto shrugged, as if to say, Okay, so what?

Indy pointed to the black tassels on the oryx's ears. "Fringe-eared . . . it's *different*."

Meto picked up his stick and touched the tip to the ears. Nodding, he said another, longer word in Maa.

"Yes!" Indy blurted. He repeated Meto's word.

Meto looked thrilled to hear Indy speaking his language. He jumped up, unleashing a torrent of words.

"Whoa . . . whoa, slow down!" Indy said in Maa.

Meto.repeated his words slowly. He touched his stick to the drawing again, then gestured to the open plain. Indy felt his heart leap. Now he understood. "Indy, I show you fringe-eared oryx!" Meto said in his slowest, clearest Maa.

With that, Meto turned and ran.

Indy clutched his notebook and took off after him. They raced across the plain, leaping over ruts and sidestepping termite hills. Way ahead of them, on the gray horizon, the flatness gave way to gently rolling foothills.

It wasn't long before they were running up one of those hills. The bushes became thicker, the trees bigger, until Indy had to lean forward and use his arms for climbing. Meto seemed to know exactly where he was going, without the slightest sign of a path to guide him.

At a wide, sunny clearing they finally stopped. Indy caught his breath and looked around. His eyes fixed on a rock wall that jutted upward like the side of a skyscraper.

In Maa, Meto said, "Oryx, up there." He gestured toward the wall.

"Up there," Indy repeated. "Good."

The rock was steep and almost sheer, except for a few crevices and bumps—but Indy couldn't wait to tackle it. He let Meto lead the way, watching him carefully dig his hands and toes into the tiniest of footholds.

Indy hoisted himself up, making sure to follow Meto exactly. He wasn't going to take chances.

Singing a strange, quiet melody to himself, Meto pulled himself up quickly. His arms and legs worked without stopping, as if he were climbing a ladder.

Indy was determined to make it. He vowed not to compete with Meto, just to stay alive. He concentrated on the rock, one hold at a time. Every muscle in his body was throbbing now, all the way down to the tips of his fingers. Just above him was a tiny crevice, which he reached for with his right hand . . .

But something else had gotten there first.

Indy gasped and pulled his hand away. The shift of weight almost ripped his body from the rock wall. With a surge of force that made every knuckle scream with pain, he held himself fast.

A pair of narrow yellow eyes leered casually down at him from the crevice. With a satisfied *hissss*, a snake began slithering toward him.

Indy hated snakes. No, it was more than that. He was deathly afraid of them, and that's all there was to it. Given a choice, he would rather be back underneath the wildebeests.

At that moment, even a seventy-foot fall seemed a reasonable alternative.

Almost.

"Meeeetooooo!" Indy shouted, his voice slicing through the dry air.

Meto's head jerked around. His eyes widened with shock. "Stop!" he said in Maa. "Don't move!"

He scrambled downward as fast as he could. Holding tightly to a ledge just above Indy, he quickly yanked his walking stick out of his belt. With the same hand, he reached for a fist-sized rock that was wedged into another crevice.

Indy's wrist tendons stood out like taut piano wires. The snake seemed to be examining them, looking for a place to bite. Indy wanted to scream, but his jaw was locked.

Meto reached down with his stick. When the point was just above the snake's tail, he gave a sharp jab.

The snake stopped. It swiveled its head around toward Meto, then slid back up the crevice.

Gritting his teeth, Meto let fly with the rock. It whizzed through the air and conked the snake squarely on the head. The snake's upper body lurched away from the rockface.

Meto took care of the lower body with a good, swift kick.

As the snake fell to the bottom of the cliff, Indy felt a shiver race from his head right out through his toes. He began to shake uncontrollably. For a moment he wondered if the snake had bitten him, given him some strange disease.

But when Meto laid a reassuring hand on his shoulder, Indy calmed down. Taking a deep breath, he reached upward with his right hand. Meto helped him climb to the ledge above. He gave Indy a look of concern.

"I'm okay," Indy said with a nod.

The two of them began climbing again. It wasn't long before Meto stopped at another ledge, big enough to support both boys.

As Indy scrambled onto it, Meto pointed to a wall directly in front of them. It was covered with drawings. The outlines were crude, but there was no mistaking the shapes of lions, wildebeests, zebras, and buffalo—and a broad-chested animal with spearlike horns and tassels on its ears.

Meto reached for the notebook tucked into Indy's belt. Riffling through the pages, he found the drawing of the fringe-eared oryx. He proudly held up Indy's drawing next to the outline on the wall. "Fringe-eared oryx!" he said in Maa.

"Yes, the fringe-eared oryx," Indy said. "But where can I *see* it?"

Meto looked at him blankly.

Indy held the binoculars to his eyes and mimed searching the landscape. "Where . . . ?" he repeated, putting his hand on the cave painting.

Meto nodded. He pondered the question solemnly, then shrugged.

"You don't understand," Indy said. "I have to find it. I promised the President."

Meto used the Maa words for "slow down," but Indy was in no mood for translating.

"I *have* to find it!" Indy repeated.

He turned to leave—but suddenly the oryx was the furthest thing from his mind. A slithering knot of snakes was headed straight for him. Closer and closer they moved, sliding rapidly over the rocks.

"Snaa-aa-ke!" yelled Indy. He grabbed Meto's arm and they raced down the steep rockface, slipping and sliding all the way.

Chapter 8

The hot African mornings were getting to Miss Seymour. She had risen at the crack of dawn, because the sun had streamed into her tent. Then, by nine, she'd been ready for a nap. It wasn't this way in England.

As she napped that morning, she slowly became aware of a rhythmic grunting noise outside her tent. Her eyes popped open. She went to the tent flap and looked out.

There was ex-President Roosevelt, tirelessly lifting a set of dumbbells. He bent his knees, stood erect, lifted the weights over his head, then reversed the movements. His glasses were sliding down his nose on a film of sweat, and his potbelly jiggled over his belt.

Still, there was something about that man. . . .

Miss Seymour glanced at her pocket timepiece, wondering how long she had slept. It was a quarter past ten o'clock.

Ten fifteen? Young Henry had been due for a Latin lesson at ten.

Miss Seymour walked over to his tent. "Henry?" she called through the flap.

No answer.

Next she went to the taxidermists' tent. Outside, Mr. Heller cheerfully worked on a rhino carcass. Miss Seymour looked inside, but there was no sign of Indy.

As she walked around back, toward the water buckets, she spotted Professor Jones and his wife a few tents to her left. "Professor?" she called out, running toward him. "I can't find Henry anywhere!"

Professor Jones furrowed his eyebrows. "When did you last see him?"

Miss Seymour thought carefully. She had seen him wandering around that morning, while she'd been fixing her hair. "About two hours ago," she said. "Maybe three."

"Perhaps he's gone exploring and has lost track of time," Mrs. Jones said, her face clouding with worry.

Miss Seymour shook her head. "Well, this is no place to go missing!"

"We'd all better split up and look," Professor Jones said.

"Oh, no . . ." Mrs. Jones was looking paler by the second.

"You check the edge of the camp," Professor Jones said to Miss Seymour, pointing to the surrounding brush. "I'll search the ridge, and Anna, you'd better look in all the tents."

Miss Seymour hiked up her long skirt and trotted to the boundary of camp. Gone exploring, yes, that was it. Typical of a ten-year-old boy who knew he had a Latin lesson. Surely he was a few yards away in the bushes, trying to follow some exotic rodent or something. She would find him there, give him a sound talking-to, then march him back to the tent for his lesson.

But as she scanned the scrubby area at the edge of the camp, she couldn't stop the flutters in her stomach.

Indy and Meto stopped at the gate of the kraal. They breathed heavily, winded from the climb down the rockface and the long run back. The early afternoon sun beat down on them fiercely, and Indy could swear he heard his sweat sizzle.

Under the watchful eyes of the dark-skinned Maasai herders, cattle ambled out through the opening in the thorn fence. Some of the animals gave Indy and Meto a brief, lazy-eyed look before moving on.

Meto smiled at the cattle, even chuckling a little when one of them swished its tail in another's face. When one of the cows gave a loud moo, a herder imitated it perfectly and laughed.

After the cattle were all out, Indy and Meto walked through the gate. Children were playing inside the kraal. Some were high-jumping over sticks and others were pretending to herd imaginary cattle. One big group was gathered around a grass-and-stick model that looked like a kraal. Inside was a collection of small rocks, which the children were moving around while making mooing sounds.

Roosevelt had been right. Clearly, the Maasai loved their cattle.

Indy looked toward one of the larger huts. Three or four of the ornately dressed warriors were staring at him now. Their spears glinted in the sun.

Indy felt the sweat prickling around his collar. He tried to keep a friendly expression on his face without looking too ridiculous.

Soon a couple of boys Meto's age came over, eying Indy suspiciously. Meto immediately took Indy's notebook and showed it to them.

They gathered around, looking at the drawing of the fringe-eared oryx. Meto spoke in rapid-fire Maa.

One of the boys nodded, then answered Meto with a short sentence. The three boys looked toward one of the huts, where three women were cooking over an open fire.

Indy followed the boys as they walked to the hut. When Meto held out the drawing and asked the women about it, they shrugged. One of them muttered something, and instantly Meto and his friends walked inside.

Indy stood there, not knowing what to do. The three women were glaring at him. Was it because he was a stranger? Were they telling him not to go in? He wished he knew more of their language.

Suddenly Meto poked his head out of the hut. He grabbed Indy by the shoulder and pulled him in.

In the center sat an old woman, cross-legged on the floor. She stared at Indy's drawing, which was laid out in front of her. Around her, Meto's friends chattered excitedly.

With a sudden shout, the old woman silenced the boys. Her eyes rose until they met Indy's. Then she smiled and said, "Hello."

A familiar word—what a shock! "You speak English?" Indy asked.

Slowly the old woman stood up. She looked Indy deeply in the eye, as if trying to read his mind.

Then she said, "No."

All three boys laughed at Indy's bewildered expression. The woman gave Indy a kind, apologetic smile, picked up his notebook, then said something to the other boys in Maa.

She began walking out of the hut, followed by the boys. Meto nodded triumphantly to Indy, gesturing for him to come.

As they all walked toward the kraal gate, Meto called to the women outside the hut. A couple of them dropped their spoons and joined the procession.

Immediately one of the young warriors ran over, as if sensing they would need protection. Four younger boys, squealing with excitement, tagged along behind him.

So there were twelve of them filing through the gate. Indy felt as if he were in a parade. Kids were trying to climb onto him for piggyback rides, everyone wanted to look through his binoculars—and no one was telling him where they were going.

Pronouncing his Maa words carefully, Indy asked Meto, "We find oryx, yes?" He pointed toward his notebook, then raised his hands to his head, pantomiming a pair of ears.

Meto nodded solemnly.

Indy smiled—but still, he had the feeling they were all on some sort of wild-goose chase. And the fringe-eared oryx was his wild goose.

But there was no turning back. By now, he figured, his parents would be worried about him. If he showed up with information about the oryx, at least Roosevelt would stick up for him. If not . . .

Indy exhaled. A smile crept across his face. It was a big animal. It couldn't stay hidden for long.

Not from Indiana Jones.

Chapter 9

As Indy trekked across the plain, his parents and Miss Seymour paced anxiously outside President Roosevelt's tent.

"Are you sure you've looked everywhere?" Roosevelt asked.

"Absolutely," Miss Seymour replied. "There is no question that he is gone."

"Perhaps he's exploring," Roosevelt suggested. "Bird-watching."

Mrs. Jones shook her head. Her eyes brimmed with tears. "God knows what's out there," she said. "He wouldn't just disappear like this un-less something had happened."

"Now, don't start getting worked up," Professor Jones said. "He can't have gone too far."

"I sincerely hope he hasn't," Roosevelt said. Then, turning toward a nearby tent, he shouted, *"Kermit!"*

Kermit poked his head out of the tent with a what-did-I-do-wrong-now? look. "Yes, Dad?"

"Get a search party together!" Roosevelt bel-lowed.

"Now?" Kermit asked.

"Now!"

As Roosevelt turned back to the others, he noticed Mrs. Jones starting to cry. "Now, don't you worry, Mrs. Jones," he said gently, "we'll find him."

Miss Seymour nodded somberly. "That's right," she said. "I'm sure Mr. Roosevelt will find him."

But as Professor Jones wrapped his wife in a reassuring embrace, she didn't look convinced.

It was midafternoon when Indy heard the soft, sweet sound of a flute. He and his new Maasai friends had been walking for more than an hour, and his head was pulsating with the heat. At first he thought the flute was in his imagination. Was there such a thing as a *sound* mirage?

The others looked as if they'd been on a short walk around the block. They danced along, joking and singing. Indy couldn't understand it. All he wanted to do was collapse into a tub of cold water.

The old woman stopped. Her gaze was fixed on a small, grassy hill directly ahead of them.

Indy could see wisps of smoke on the hilltop. Through squinted eyes, he spotted the outline of a man sitting against a tree and playing the flute. A small fire burned on the ground next to him.

"Laibon," the old woman said. She held up the picture of the fringe-eared oryx and nodded in the man's direction.

At that moment it became clear to Indy what this trek was all about. The Laibon must be some kind of wise, respected person in the tribe. Maybe he was the one who knew about the fringe-eared oryx.

As they climbed the hill, the Maasai fell silent. One by one they sat down quietly in a semicircle around the Laibon.

The old man slowly lowered his flute. His dark-brown face was deeply lined and leathery from a long life in the sun. His eyes pierced brightly through the shadow of his brow. He gave Indy a quick glance, not more than a split second. Despite the heat, Indy felt a sudden chill. It was as if the Laibon had sized him up, figured out every angle of his personality instantly.

Indy pointed to the drawing in his notebook, then looked around exaggeratedly as if trying to find something.

The woman offered the open notebook to the Laibon. He unclasped his gnarled fingers from the flute and took it.

He stared at the drawing for what seemed like ages, then nodded. Looking up slowly, he said the Maa phrase for "fringe-eared oryx."

"Yes, fringe-eared oryx," Indy replied in Maa. "Where?"

The Laibon said nothing for a moment. Then he bent forward and used his right hand to sweep smooth a patch of dirt in front of him. Looking up, he said something to Meto.

Meto sprang to his feet, twisted a twig off the tree, and gave it to the old man.

Slowly the Laibon drew a straight, horizontal line in the dirt. Then he patted the ground and said a Maa word.

Indy remembered that the word meant "earth." He repeated it.

The Laibon nodded, then drew a circle just under the line. From the top of the circle, he drew another straight line, pointing upward.

Indy shook his head and shrugged.

The old man answered with a pantomime. First he made a digging motion with his hands, pretending to take something round out of the earth. Then he put his hands to his mouth and mimed eating.

After he finished, he said a Maa word.

Something edible in the ground. But what? And what did it have to do with the fringe-eared oryx?

Indy shrugged again.

The Laibon began to draw a crude stick figure of an animal on top of the straight line. Its head was down, as if it were grazing.

Then it hit him. "Something the oryx eats—a root?" Indy blurted out.

The old woman's face lit up. "Root melon," she said in English. Then she repeated it in Maa. "Root melon!"

The others nodded happily and began chattering among themselves.

Pointing to his fire, the Laibon said another word.

Fire . . . oryx eating a melon . . . Indy tried to put the clues together. Roosevelt had said the fringe-eared oryx used to live in this area. That meant the melon grew here. Indy didn't remember seeing any melons growing, but that really meant nothing.

"Laibon," Indy said in English, "did the fire wipe out the root melons?"

The Laibon gave him a baffled look. Indy repeated the Maa word for "fire," pointed to the drawing of the melon, and wiped it out.

The Laibon understood. He shook his head no. As he drew more pictures and pantomimed more details, Indy took notes. Snakes were involved in some way. Mole rats, too. It was pretty complicated, and Indy wasn't sure he grasped it all. But one thing was clear: Somehow the melons disappeared. And when they did, so did the fringe-eared oryx.

Indy was concentrating so hard, he didn't notice the excited expression on Meto's face. Nor did he see his friend suddenly scamper down the hill and sprint away into the distance.

"I think I see now," Indy said when he finished writing. "If we find this melon, we'll find the fringe-eared oryx."

He looked at the Laibon. The old man couldn't have understood what Indy had said, but he seemed to sense that Indy was satisfied. For the first time, he smiled.

"Thank you," Indy said as he closed the notebook and stood up. "Thank you very much!"

He held out his hand to the Laibon. The old man held it gently for a moment, then picked up his flute and began playing again.

The Maasai sang along to the tune, dancing joyously. But Meto wasn't with them.

"Meto?" Indy said softly.

He looked around, but his friend was nowhere to be seen. That was when Indy noticed that the sun was already setting.

"Gosh, it's late!" he said. "I have to get back!"

Alone, Indy started running down the hill.

At camp, Anna Jones couldn't sit down. The sun was now a fierce orange sliver on the horizon, and soon it would be gone. With darkness, the search would have to be called off, and her son would spend the night alone in the wilderness.

No—he wouldn't be alone, really. Not if you counted the lions and buffalo and wildebeests.

Mrs. Jones fought to keep back her tears. Indy had always been capable. He had always managed to take care of himself. Surely he'd find a way back.

At the sound of approaching hooves, her hopes rose. Judging by the noise, there were quite a few horses coming down the hill behind the camp. She ran to meet them, as did most of the tribesmen who had remained behind.

Professor Jones and President Roosevelt were the first to arrive. Behind them were a few askaris and gun bearers, but no Indy.

Mrs. Jones looked into her husband's eyes for a glimmer of good news.

Professor Jones shook his head. "We can't find him anywhere."

"Maybe he's found somewhere safe," she said, more like a question than a statement.

"I hope so," Roosevelt replied. He turned to the tribesmen and called out, "Make a big fire at the top of the hill."

The men rushed off. Mrs. Jones wondered if that fire could warm the chill she felt inside.

*   *   *

It was a good thing Indy's mom couldn't see where he was right then. It was an even better thing she didn't know how he felt.

Terrified.

Somewhere in the East African grassland, Indy ran for his life. He had long since given up trying to guess where he was. All he knew was that he was somewhere between the camp, the kraal, Europe, and Antarctica. The sun had set, and it was getting darker and darker. Indy had no idea what was under his feet or what lurked around him. His only reliable sense was his hearing—and that wasn't filling him with hope.

To his left he thought he heard a snarl, to his right a snapping of branches. All around him, the bushes seemed to be hiding huge animal shapes. Or were those shapes just bushes? Indy didn't want to stop and find out.

Panic made his heart race. His legs pounded the ground, as if his muscles had forgotten they were ever tired. Thorns lashed his face and tore at his clothes. Tiny black rodents skittered across his pathway, squeaking with fright.

Why did I have to do this? a voice screamed inside Indy's mind. Who cares about a dumb fringe-eared oryx and its stupid melon? He thought about Meto and felt the blood rising to his head. Where *was* Meto? Why did he disappear? Was this some kind of cruel joke?

Indy felt a shooting pain in his foot. It was caught—in what? A hole? A root? Indy had no time to wonder. His body hurtled forward. His arms shot out to break his fall. He braced himself for the pain.

But he never reached the ground. Something stopped him. Something bigger than Indy—and very, very much alive.

Chapter 10

Indy went blank. His breath left him in a gush, his eyes saw nothing. He was aware of being lifted, then placed upright on the ground.

When his vision cleared, Indy found himself staring into two eyes that were like white pools in the darkness.

No mane.

No snout.

No fur.

Those were the first thoughts that shot through Indy's brain. Whatever stopped him was not an animal. He was face to face with a human being.

He should have felt relieved, but he didn't. Who knew what tribe this guy belonged to, what language he spoke. Indy struggled to remember the Maa word for "Hello," but somehow when he thought of "Maa" he thought of his mother, and all he wanted to do was call for her.

But there was something happening under the eyes. Something that looked suspiciously like a smile. "Henry?" the man said.

Indy gave him a blank look.

"Askari," the man said. He patted a rifle that was slung around his shoulder. "Mr. Roosevelt safari."

"You—you're an—?" Indy stammered.

The askari threw his head back in laughter. "I scare you?" he said, as if it were the funniest thing he'd heard all day.

Indy's fear vanished. He didn't know whether to laugh or collapse with fatigue.

"Come, I take you back," the askari said. "Everybody miss you."

They walked toward a distant hill, on top of which glowed a pale orange fire. Gray smoke rose in a plume against the black sky.

As they came closer, Indy saw a familiar silhouette flickering in the firelight. Indy smiled as the silhouette began running down the hill, its skirt billowing around its legs.

"Mom?" Indy called out.

In seconds his mother reached him. Even in the darkness he could see she'd been crying. She wrapped him in a long, long hug. Then she pulled him back, looking him over with relief and concern.

When she saw he was all right, anger suddenly flared in her eyes and she shook him by the shoulders. "Don't ever, *ever* do that again. We've been worried sick!"

"I'm sorry, Mom," Indy replied softly.

Mrs. Jones thanked the askari. Then the three of them walked back over the hill to camp.

Professor Jones and Mr. Roosevelt were standing by a campfire. As Indy approached they said nothing. Indy tried a smile, but neither of them smiled back.

The expression on his dad's face made Indy wish, for a moment, that he were back in the wilderness. But it was Roosevelt who spoke first. "You've caused more than enough trouble for one day, Henry. I'm disappointed in you. I thought you were more intelligent."

"But sir," Indy protested, "I've been looking for the fringe-eared oryx. I just lost track of time—"

"No excuses!" Roosevelt snapped. Turning to Indy's dad, he added, "Professor Jones, I suggest you keep a closer eye on your son in the future. The African bush is no playground!"

Roosevelt stalked away. Professor Jones's angry face was now red with embarrassment.

Indy looked downward. This was one of the most awful days of his life. He had failed in his mission to find the oryx, been abandoned by his only African friend, and gotten his parents furious.

But that was nothing compared with the worst thing of all. He had let his hero down.

"I'm sorry," Indy said in a small voice.

"So you should be!" Professor Jones retorted. "You are going straight to bed, and no supper for you, my lad!"

Indy obediently turned around and walked to his tent. No supper probably meant no fried wildebeest, which wasn't so bad. But from the way his stomach was growling, any meat would do. He was starving, and he'd stay that way till morning. It was just one more disappointment in a horrendous day.

Inside the tent, Indy flopped onto his cot. He felt the bulge of his notebook in his pocket. Getting up, he lit a kerosene lamp and laid the notebook on his bed.

He opened to the picture of the fringe-eared oryx and looked at his notes. He began thinking furiously, trying to piece together what the Laibon had said. He had to be able to tell President Roosevelt how the fringe-eared oryx had disappeared . . . if it really had! Were there some still around? And if there were, how could he find them? Indy searched for some clue, some new way of looking at this.

Slowly, slowly, it all started to come together. The more Indy thought, the clearer it became. The root melon . . . a fire . . . snakes . . . mole rats . . . Indy began scribbling in his notebook, jotting down his thoughts as quickly as he could.

But soon his eyes were closing, and he couldn't fight them for long. He shut the book, dropped it on the floor, and went to sleep.

When Indy heard the noise outside, he was in the middle of a dream. His eyes popped open. It could have been five minutes since he'd fallen asleep, or five hours. All Indy knew for sure was that it was still dark, and no one in the camp should have been wandering around.

Scritch, scritch . . . It sounded close. Too close. Indy lay still. The last thing he wanted to do was attract its attention.

There was a movement across one side of the tent. It was barely visible in the moonlight, and then it was gone. The noise stopped. Indy heard only the lazy chittering of insects. Whatever it was had moved on.

Indy couldn't relax. What if it was headed for another tent? What if it decided to attack his parents?

He pulled aside his covers, determined to find something heavy he could use as a weapon. But before his feet hit the ground, the tent flap flew open.

Indy dived under the cot. Something came closer. Indy could feel it leaning on the cot. He tensed his muscles, ready to push the cot upward.

"In-dee."

Indy froze at the sound of the voice. "Meto!" he said with disbelief.

In hushed but excited Maa, Meto said, "Come! We find oryx!"

Indy couldn't believe his ears. How could Meto

expect Indy to trust him after the way he'd disappeared this afternoon? How could he sneak into the tent and expect Indy would just pick up and go? Besides, if Indy ever left camp again without permission, his parents would ground him till he was thirty! "I can't—" Indy began.

But Meto cut him off. "Melon!" he said in Maa. "Fringe-eared oryx! Come see!"

Indy came out from under the cot. "Are you sure?" he asked, not bothering to think of the Maa words.

Meto nodded. He was practically dancing with excitement. Gesturing for Indy to follow, he left the tent.

Indy didn't allow himself to think. All his doubts were put aside. He quickly rolled up some blankets and pillows and arranged them under his sheets in a roughly human shape. Then he put on his shoes and ran after Meto.

The pre-dawn light made the plain seem an eerie silver-gray. Overhead the flying birds looked liquid against the sky. There was no distant roaring or bellowing in the bush; there were no twitters or tweets or squawks or snorts. Just the muffled, overlapping *pat-pat-pat* of two pairs of feet as Indy and Meto ran full tilt toward the foothills.

The plain ended in an area of thick bushes and trees. There, the boys had to slow down, pushing aside vines and branches that reached toward them like spidery arms.

A high-pitched shriek from above made Indy's hair stand on end. He looked up. Black-and-white-striped monkeys were swinging wildly from tree to tree. One of them screamed again, baring its teeth and looking straight at Indy.

Indy felt Meto's hand grabbing his arm. "Come on!" Meto urged in Maa.

They continued onward. With each step, the animal sounds seemed to increase around them, and Meto seemed to move faster. Indy had the feeling they were running out of time.

The land began sloping upward. For the second time in twenty-four hours, Indy and Meto were climbing a steep hill. For the second time, they emerged from the bush into a clearing.

But this clearing had no sheer rockface on the far side. Instead, it ended in a long, rocky, upward-sloping ledge. In the distance, far beyond the ledge, Indy could see the mountainous outline of the East African highlands. But between the ledge and the highlands the land dropped out of sight.

Meto and Indy ran to the end of the ledge and looked over. The sight took Indy's breath away. Shimmering in the silvery light was a small valley, like some enchanted, tucked-away land. The ground was covered with green. Lush, leafy trees spread their branches over small, still watering holes. Gazelles pranced through the brush, stopping now and then to graze.

The boys scrabbled down the front of the ledge. At the valley floor, Meto led Indy to an area where straggly stalks grew out of the ground. Frantically Meto began digging with his hands at the base of a stalk.

Indy knelt down to help. The two boys brushed away the surface dirt, revealing something round and smooth underneath.

Indy felt a surge of energy. In no time they uncovered a hard, round object, a little smaller than a football. They pulled it out of the ground and held it up.

Some melon, Indy thought. This thing was more like a giant turnip—tough and dull-colored and solid. Like a *root*. At least that part of the description was right.

Well, whatever it was—root, turnip, melon—

they had found it! The two boys exchanged a knowing smile. "So now we wait . . ." Indy said, watching the sky slowly turn pink with the dawn.

Across the plain, the aroma of coffee and fried meat drifted over Roosevelt's safari camp. Mrs. Jones, in her nightclothes and a robe, tiptoed over to her son's tent. Pulling the flap aside, she looked inside.

It was dark, but the bed was definitely full. Under the blanket, all four feet plus of young Indiana Jones seemed to be fast asleep. That was all that counted.

She smiled and walked away. The poor little guy was probably exhausted. She'd let him lie there as long as he wanted.

Chapter 11

They came with the sun.

There was a rustle in the bushes the moment the valley turned red-orange with the sunrise. The first of the animals poked its head through the bush. Its nostrils opened and closed, and it stepped into the area where the root melons were growing. One by one, three other oryxes walked in behind it.

From deep within the surrounding bush, Indy looked through his binoculars. He couldn't take his eyes off the animals' spear-like horns. They seemed impossibly long. They sliced and jabbed the air as the animals dug at the roots with their hooves and snouts.

Still Indy wasn't sure if this was the right species. The beisa oryx had horns like this, and so did the gemsbok.

The light was still fairly dim, and the animals were moving their heads quickly. Indy tried to focus on the ears.

The first animal lifted its head. It seemed to be eating the root melon, chewing contentedly. Several flies began buzzing around it, and the oryx gave its head a sudden twitch, flicking its ears downward.

And that was when Indy saw the swish of the black tuft. It was there, all right, sprouting out of the top of the ear like some huge set of false eyelashes.

Indy felt like shouting with joy, but there was no way he was going to scare off these oryxes. He wanted them to stay here as long as possible—long enough for him to carry out the plan that was forming in his head.

For now, he shared a silent but ecstatic smile with Meto. And that was enough.

*   *   *

By the time Indy and Meto got back to the camp, breakfast was almost over. Without saying a word, the two boys split up. Indy headed for the dining hut, and Meto hid behind an empty tent, clutching the melon they'd dug up.

Step One of Indy's plan had begun.

Pausing outside the dining hut, Indy caught his breath. He tucked his shirt neatly into his pants and tried hard to look well rested.

With a contented yawn, he strolled into the hut and sat next to his mom.

"Good morning, dear," Mrs. Jones said warmly.

Across the table, Miss Seymour was sitting next to Roosevelt. She looked very cheerful as she added her own "Good morning."

"Morning," Indy replied. "Pass the wildebeest, please."

Mr. Selous passed a serving plate of steak and eggs to Professor Jones, who passed it silently to Indy.

At the head of the table President Roosevelt swallowed deeply, then said, "Lechwe today. Not wildebeest."

"*Lechwe?*" Indy smiled. "You mean it?"

Roosevelt looked puzzled. "Yes, it's a type of antelope. Why?"

Indy choked back a laugh, remembering how the animal's name had bewildered him and his dad on the steamship. "Just curious."

Scowling, Roosevelt said, "Well, I hope you learned your lesson last night, Henry."

"Yes, I did, sir," Indy replied.

"Bully for you," Roosevelt said, wiping his chin. "Now, if you all will excuse me . . ."

He got up to leave, but someone was blocking the way out.

Meto.

Indy rolled his eyes. This wasn't in the plan. Meto was supposed to wait. The whole thing was supposed to be more . . . *subtle.* Indy sighed. This would just have to do.

"Excuse me," Roosevelt grumbled.

But Meto didn't move. Nervously hoisting the melon in the air, he called out, "Indy, Indy!"

Roosevelt gave Meto a quizzical glance. He stepped aside as Meto rushed toward Indy.

"What the devil . . ." Mr. Selous said. "Vegetables for breakfast?"

"Here's the melon," Meto blurted in Maa as he handed it to Indy. "Tell them! Tell them!"

Indy answered him in Maa. "Slow down. Take it easy!"

Miss Seymour looked surprised. "I don't recognize that language . . ."

"What is he saying?" Mrs. Jones asked.

Taking a deep breath, Indy said, "This is Meto. He's my friend and he's been helping me. I tried to tell you all yesterday—we've found the fringe-eared oryx."

Roosevelt, who was almost out of the hut, turned around.

"They're across the plain," Indy said matter-of-factly. Then he handed the melon to his dad. "It's the root melon, you see."

Professor Jones looked at the melon blankly. "I don't understand."

"Let me see," Mrs. Jones asked, rising to get a closer look.

"Well, well," Selous said, peering at the melon through his spectacles. Miss Seymour, too, stood up to examine it.

Out of the corner of his eye, Indy saw Roosevelt coming nearer. Good. He was getting curious.

Indy's confidence began to grow. "The fringe-eared oryxes aren't here anymore because they like to feed on this kind of root melon." He added the Maa word for "root melon," looking directly at Roosevelt.

Roosevelt was walking back to the table now. He was all ears.

"I recognize it," Selous piped up. "We call those melons 'elephant footballs.' "

"Meto here helped me find out what happened," Indy said to Roosevelt. "I promised you I'd find them, and I have. It's all written down here."

He pulled his notebook out of his pocket, open to the notes he had furiously scribbled down the night before. Then he handed the book to Roosevelt.

"You see," Indy said, "there was a great fire in the bush, which killed all the snakes. These snakes usually ate the mole rats—"

"—But the mole rats burrowed underground and survived the fire," Roosevelt read aloud.

"Right!" Indy said. "With no snakes to eat the mole rats, there got to be so many of them, they ate all the melons. No root melons, no oryx!"

Wide-eyed, Roosevelt took the root melon from Professor Jones and examined it.

"You see," Indy explained, "all the plants and animals are connected. Anything that happens to one animal causes things to happen to other animals. The oryx moved away to find the root melons."

"Very perceptive, Henry," Miss Seymour said with a smile.

"This is a curious melon," Mrs. Jones remarked.

"Actually, it grows underground," Indy said. "The oryxes dig it up. I guess it's called a melon because of its shape."

"Obviously." Professor Jones harrumphed. "And what about the oryx?"

"Meto and I saw them!" Indy replied. "Only a few—but they're the most beautiful animals!" Looking at Roosevelt, he shrugged. "That's why I lost track of time . . . yesterday."

Indy felt a little guilty adding that last word, but it didn't seem to matter. Roosevelt's eyes were dancing with excitement. "How far did you say?"

"It's a small valley," Indy said, pointing in the general direction where he and Meto had just been, "in the middle of the bush, over that way."

Indy could feel his dad staring at him. His all-knowing eyes seemed to be saying, You got away with it this time, didn't you?

"You have a very bright lad here, Professor

Jones," Roosevelt proclaimed. Then he called to his saise, "Saddle up! And get some horses for my friends here!"

The saise hopped into action. Selous ran into the gun tent, followed by Professor Jones. And Mrs. Jones examined the root melon with Miss Seymour.

Meto and Indy grinned. They didn't need words to tell each other exactly how they felt.

Chapter 12

The sun was streaming into the valley as the horses pulled up on the ledge. All of the riders—Indy, Meto, Roosevelt, Selous, Professor Jones, and Kermit—took a breather, staring in awe at the green-drenched beauty below.

Meto led them down to a secluded spot slightly above the melon plants. There, they all dismounted and hitched their horses to trees. Selous began unloading the rifles from their leather carriers.

"You sure this is the place?" Roosevelt whispered to Indy.

Indy was ready to burst with anticipation. "Yes, sir," he said, about ten decibels too loud. He looked at Meto, who was beaming with pride.

"Let's go, then," Roosevelt said.

Selous gave three rifles to Professor Jones. "You're elected gun bearer, my friend," he said.

Professor Jones forced a smile. Indy could tell his dad wasn't thrilled by the idea.

Together Meto and Indy led the others forward. They found the hiding place they had used only hours before. Through the bushes, Indy pointed to the melon stalks.

Immediately Roosevelt, Kermit, and Selous took their rifles from Professor Jones. Quietly they settled into shooting positions in the bush, their sights trained on the stalks.

Indy's eyes flashed to the now familiar area. He hoped the oryxes would appear. He pictured them twitching their ears, shaking their regal heads as the points of their spear-horns drew patterns in the air.

Then Indy looked back at the three hunters. "Are you *all* going to shoot?" he asked.

"Shhh!" Roosevelt hissed.

Indy fell silent. He had led them all here. He had almost gotten himself killed in his search, and he had been proud of his sleuthing. But he'd been so busy he hadn't stopped to think.

He hadn't really thought of what would happen in the end.

Time passed. It felt like three hours but was probably more like ten minutes. Then there was a heavy rustling in the brush near the melon stalks. The hunters tightened their stances.

Indy felt his gut clench. He had wanted desperately to show he'd been right about the oryxes, but something inside him now hoped a zebra would emerge, or a buffalo. Anything but a fringe-eared oryx.

But there was no mistaking the horns. And the ear tufts were vivid in the light of day. One by one the animals stepped into the clearing where the stalks were, until there were at least six of them, all eager for another feast.

"Here we go . . ." Kermit whispered.

Each of the three men followed an oryx in his sight.

Meto put his fingers in his ears.

Indy stared, unable to move a muscle.

Crrrrrrraaaack!

Roosevelt got off the first shot. The oryx had no time to react. It jerked backward and fell to the ground.

Three of the other oryxes just stood there, frozen with shock. Two more started dancing and kicking. Only one tried to run back into the bush.

Crrrrrrraaaack! Crrrrrrraaaack!

Kermit and Selous fired quickly. One of the standing oryxes fell in a heap. The escaping oryx collapsed at the edge of the clearing.

Three down.

Indy's jaw fell open. This wasn't what he'd planned.

Roosevelt took aim again. He lined up one of the bucking animals in his sight . . . waiting for the right moment.

Thoughts raced through Indy's mind.

Beasts such as these belong in a museum for everyone to share. . . . There are hundreds of museums. That was what Roosevelt had said. Was he thinking of which museum he would send each oryx to? Would there be enough to go around? Was he going to keep shooting until he got them all?

But Roosevelt had said something else too: *Always remember, a gun should only be used in order to survive.*

Indy remembered being confused by Roosevelt's two very different statements. But he wasn't confused now. Right now no one was using a gun to survive. And those beautiful animals did not deserve to sit dead and stuffed in a museum case.

Indy sprang into furious action. He leaped at Roosevelt, pushing the gun barrel away. "No more!" he screamed.

Roosevelt wheeled around. His face was bright red, his teeth clenched with rage.

A few minutes ago, that look would have scared the daylights out of Indy. But he was beyond fear now. "I said no more!" he shouted.

Kermit and Mr. Selous lowered their guns. They stared at Indy, their eyes wide with disbelief.

"You've killed too many!" Indy went on. "No more!"

His words echoed through the valley. As they died away, the only other sound was the frantic hoofbeats of the remaining oryxes running for safety.

In seconds that sound was gone, too. The clearing was empty except for the three fallen animals.

Indy saw nothing but the eyes of the greatest living American president. They were glaring at him in murderous fury, distorted by the sweat-streaked lenses of his glasses. For a moment, Indy felt as trapped as those oryxes. He backed away, waiting for Roosevelt to explode.

A bead of sweat grew on the President's left eyebrow. It fell to his cheek and merged with a small patch of wetness there.

The cheek lifted, sending the patch in a small cascade down Roosevelt's face. Wrinkles formed at the sides of his eyes.

It took Indy a moment to realize that Roosevelt was smiling.

"Quite right, too," came Roosevelt's voice. "You're absolutely right, Henry. Might be a rare species. Who knows what animals depend on them being around, eh?"

Indy heard the words. He knew that Roosevelt was saying them. But Roosevelt wasn't important right now. Indy turned his head toward the clearing.

Meto was kneeling beside one of the blood-soaked oryxes. Shock and sadness etched his face as he cradled the twisted corpse and tried to lift its head up.

Indy looked away. His eye caught some movement in the distance. Glancing up, he saw a line of animals racing up the other side of the valley.

As they disappeared, the last things he saw were their long, pointed horns. He felt a small sense of relief.

He snapped back to reality when a heavy hand landed on his shoulder. He looked up into President Roosevelt's face. "Thank you, Henry," Roosevelt said softly.

Indy moved away. "Yes, sir."

He wasn't sure, but as he quietly walked back to his horse, he thought he heard Roosevelt add: "Bully for you!"

Chapter 13

The next day Indy peeked over the ridge near camp, his binoculars dangling from his neck. Sure enough, there were Meto and his goats, in their usual spot. "Meto!" he called out.

Meto looked up as Indy ran toward him. He called out a greeting in Maa.

When Indy reached him, he took a deep breath and said, "We're going now." He mimed a walking-away motion with his fingers. "Going."

Meto's face grew somber. He nodded.

Indy took the binoculars from around his neck. They had been a gift from his first hero on the trip, and now they were going to be a gift to his last hero.

He placed them over Meto's head and said the Maa word for oryx.

Meto smiled proudly. He had a gift, too. Reaching into a leather pouch, he pulled out his flute and handed it to Indy. It was the same one he and Indy had played a few days earlier, and now Indy realized it was exactly like the one the Laibon had played.

Indy put it to his lips and again tried to play a tune.

Again it sounded horrible.

The two boys burst out laughing. Indy wondered at the fairness of this deal. Binoculars were easy to use, but playing the Maasai flute was nearly impossible.

Indy thought of the Laibon, of how simply he played such beautiful melodies. It occurred to Indy he had never told the Laibon *why* he was searching for the oryx. He had been in such a feverish rush to find it, the *why* had seemed unimportant.

Maybe if he had told everything, the Laibon would have warned him, or lied in order to keep

Indy away. Then none of the oryxes would have been killed.

Then again, maybe the Laibon knew what Indy had in mind. Maybe he wanted Indy to experience the consequences, to learn for himself.

Indy thanked Meto and said good-bye.

He hoped he'd see Meto again. Maybe next time there would be big herds of fringe-eared oryxes in British East Africa. Maybe someday he and Meto would climb a hilltop, lean against a gnarled tree, and watch them stampede across the plain.

Indy tucked the flute into his belt and turned back to the camp. It was time to face reality— Miss Seymour wanted him to make up that Latin lesson before they left.

But Miss Seymour hadn't arrived at Indy's desk yet, so he walked to her tent. "Miss Seymour?" he called out. "I'm ready."

There was no answer, so he peered in. Suddenly he heard a laugh behind him. The voice was familiar, but the *laugh* wasn't.

He turned to see Miss Seymour walking toward the opposite edge of camp, a gun under her right arm. President Roosevelt was next to her, talking away, and Indy could just make out his words: "Fox Number Twelve shotgun . . . no better gun was ever made!"

Indy let out a whoop. As long as Theodore Roosevelt was around, even Miss Seymour knew what was most important!

Historical Note

By the time of the African safari, Teddy Roosevelt was overweight, blind in one eye, and suffering from rheumatism and occasional asthma. Some of his native porters called him "Bwana Tumbo," or "Mister Stomach"—behind his back, of course. But none of that stopped him from personally shooting 296 game animals, including 9 lions, 8 elephants, 13 rhinoceroses, 20 zebras, and 6 buffaloes. (All told, the safari, which began in March 1909 and ended in June 1910, sent back to the Smithsonian 4,900 mammals, 4,000 birds, 500 fish, and

2,000 reptiles.) Roosevelt, who was then fifty, threw himself into the safari with an energy that astounded people half his age.

Doing astounding things was nothing new for Roosevelt. He'd been doing them all his life. Born in 1858, he was a fragile, scrawny boy, constantly sick with asthma. But he devoted himself to vigorous exercise and outdoor activities, eventually becoming a boxer and body-builder. Although he never grew taller than 5'8", he made himself robust and powerful. He studied with the same zeal, finishing near the top of his class at Harvard College. While attending Columbia Law School, his idea of a vacation was to climb the 15,000-foot Matterhorn in Switzerland.

At age twenty-three, Roosevelt decided to enter politics. In his first election he became a New York state assemblyman. Three years later, after the death of his wife and mother, he left politics and moved to the Dakota Territory to run a ranch. For two years he developed his hunting and riding skills, and started forming his ideas about conservation.

He returned to public life in 1889 and became known as a crusader against corruption and as a fiery speaker. He was appointed police commissioner of New York City in 1895, then rose to assistant secretary of the Navy under President William McKinley. In 1898, he resigned to organize the First Volunteer Cavalry for the Spanish-American War's Cuban campaign. Roosevelt's exploits in Cuba made him legendary; his cavalry was nicknamed the Rough Riders.

Roosevelt returned a hero and was elected governor of New York, then vice president of the United States. When McKinley was assassinated in 1901, Roosevelt became president. In 1904, he was elected in his own right.

As president, Roosevelt was most proud of his role in conservation. In 1905, he established the United States Forest Service. His legislation expanded the national forest by some forty million acres and established four national game preserves, fifty-one national bird sanctuaries, and twenty-one national parks and monuments.

Roosevelt read an extraordinary number of books, sometimes two or three a day. He also wrote twenty-eight books, about 150,000 letters, and thousands of articles and speeches. He was an expert in world history, literature, and natural history. His African safari was one of the last adventures he undertook. In 1919, at age 60, he died in his sleep.

In the years during and after Roosevelt's safari, Africa became a growing patchwork of European colonies. By the mid-1920s, nearly all of the African continent was under foreign control. But by the 1960s, native Africans had gained independence in most countries. In 1963, British East Africa became the independent state of Kenya.

Throughout Africa today, wild country remains, but much of it has been set aside as game preserves and is heavily trafficked by automobile tours. Years of constant hunting and poaching have taken a heavy toll. Many species of game animals have become endangered, and hunting them is now illegal in many areas. If Teddy Roosevelt were alive today, his hunting habits would not be nearly so reckless. But in the time he lived, there were so many animals in Africa that one couldn't have imagined how quickly they would disappear.

The fringe-eared oryx, otherwise known by the scientific name *Oryx gazella callotis*, can still be found, especially in the south and east of Kenya. Contrary to this tale, Theodore Roosevelt's records do not show that he ever killed one.

TO FIND OUT MORE . . .

Kenya by Zachery Winslow. Published by Chelsea House, 1987. What happened to British East Africa after Indy left? Find out in this up-close look at the history, land, and peoples of Kenya. Map and photographs, many in color.

Don't You Dare Shoot That Bear! by Robert Quackenbush. Published by Simon and Schuster, 1984. A short but fact-packed biography of Indy's hero, Teddy Roosevelt, filled with lively tales from his boyhood through his presidency. Cartoon-like illustrations.

Bully for You, Teddy Roosevelt! by Jean Fritz. Published by G. P. Putnam's Sons, 1991. A riveting biography of Teddy Roosevelt. Tracks his early days as an asthmatic child, through his glory days as president, and beyond. Amusing anecdotes of this one-of-a-kind character who lived life to the fullest. Includes notes, bibliography, and illustrations.

African Game Trails by Theodore Roosevelt. First published in 1910; reissued by St. Martin's Press in 1988. Here's the true story of Roosevelt's safari to Africa, told by Teddy himself. It really captures the spirit of his 1909–10 Smithsonian expedition to Africa. Roosevelt's comments about race are unenlightened by today's standards, but his views on conservation were generally ahead of his time. The book includes a map of the safari route and pages of black-and-white photographs of African wildlife.

Growing Up Masai by Tom Shachtman. Published by Macmillan, 1981. Meet Meto's people—the Masai—in this photo essay filled with beautiful black-and-white photographs. Shows the history, traditions, and day-to-day life of this cattle-herding tribe.

When Hippo Was Hairy by Nick Greaves. Published by Barron's, 1988. A colorful collection of wildlife facts and animal tales from African mythology. Maps, glossary, and color and black-and-white illustrations. (Unfortunately, the fringe-eared oryx is not included.)

The Flame Trees of Thika by Elspeth Huxley. First published in 1959; paperback published by Penguin. A fascinating autobiography of a young girl's life on an African coffee plantation in the early 1900s. Filled with vivid descriptions of the land and peoples that Indy encountered in British East Africa. A fun read.

African Folktales: Traditional Stories of the Black World edited by Roger D. Abrahams. Published by Pantheon, 1983. Indy may have heard some of these stories around the campfire! This spirited collection of folktales for older readers celebrates Africa's diverse cultures and storytelling tradition.

THE LUCASFILM

FAN CLUB

There's a world of adventure awaiting you when you join the official Lucasfilm Fan Club!

Go behind-the-scenes on the new television series *The Young Indiana Jones Chronicles* in each issue of the quarterly Lucasfilm Fan Club Magazine. Exclusive Interviews with the cast and crew, exciting full-color photos and more fill every page! In addition, the latest news on the new *Star Wars* movies is found within the pages of the Lucasfilm Fan Club Magazine as well as interviews with actors, directors, producers, etc. from past Lucasfilm productions, special articles and photos on the special effects projects at Industrial Light & Magic, the latest in computer entertainment from Lucasfilm Games and More! Plus you'll receive, with each issue, our exclusive Lucasfilm Merchandise catalog filled with all the latest hard-to-find collectibles from *Star Wars* to *The Young Indiana Jones Chronicles* including special offers for fan club members only!

If you love the kind of entertainment only Lucasfilm can create, then The Lucasfilm Fan Club is definitely for YOU! But a one-year subscription to the Lucasfilm Fan Club Magazine is not all you receive! Join now and we'll have delivered right to your front door our brand new, exclusive *Young Indiana Jones Chronicles* Membership Kit which includes:
• Full-color poster of 16 year-old Indy, Sean Patrick Flanery!
• Full-color poster of 9 year-old Indy, Corey Carrier!
• *Young Indiana Jones Chronicles* Sticker!
• *Young Indiana Jones Chronicles* Patch!
• Welcome Letter from George Lucas!
• Lucasfilm Fan Club Membership Card

Don't miss this opportunity to be a part of the adventure and excitement that Lucasfilm creates! Join The Lucasfilm Fan Club today!

JOIN FOR ONLY $9.95

YES, SIGN ME UP FOR THE ADVENTURE! I WANT TO JOIN THE LUCASFILM FAN CLUB!

Enclosed is a check or money order for $ _____

U.S. DOLLARS ONLY; 1 YEAR MEMBERSHIP— (9.95 US) ($12.00 CANADA) ($21.95 FOREIGN)

Charge to my: ❑ Visa ❑ MasterCard

Account # _____

Signature _____

Name (please print) _____

Address _____

City/State/Zip/Country _____

Send check, money order or MC/VISA order to:
The Lucasfilm Fan Club
P.O. BOX 111000
AURORA, COLORADO 80042 USA

© & TM 1992 Lucasfilm Ltd.